The Book of Dreams

The Life Story of a Teenage Girl

To Kayce
Love,
Grandma
12/05

The Book of Dreams

The Life Story of a Teenage Girl

By Ashley Boettcher

Published By: ALB Books
P.O. Box 997 Southwick, Ma.
01077-0997 USA
www.ALBbooks.com

Chapter 42 title quote taken from "purpose Driven® Life, The"
by Rick Warren. Copyright © 2002 by Rick Warren. Used with
permission of Zondervan corporation.

Scripture taken from the New King James Version®
Copyright© 1982 by Thomas Nelson, inc. Used by permission. All
rights reserved

Chapters 2, 3, 7, 10, 11, 13, 15, 17, 21, 23, 24, 26, 27, 28, 30, 33, 35,
& 41 are used and gathered from authors own knowledge, and every
effort has been taken to give credit to the cites and their author.

Printed and Bound in the USA

For Emily, my best friend… My true inspiration!

~ Acknowledgements ~

I would like to thank Emily Drewes, for her extensive help in creating this book, and for a listening ear. For my sister, Aimee, and her smarty remarks that made Morgan Parker herself. For Bryan Parks, his prayers and support in being there. For my Mom, and my family, for their financial help and assistance during the publishing.

Thanks to Southwoods for the superb job of creating the cover graphic, and the countless thousands of copies I had made for advertising!

Also, for the dreamers who dream along with me too… This is for you.

To Joyce

~ A Note from the Author ~

The words of this book are an inspired thought. They aren't inspired by TV, they aren't inspired by another book, or even a person I admire.

This book is inspired by God, and everything in it I placed in His hands from the very beginning. God used people, He used experiences, but most of all,
He used me.

To God be the glory. Enjoy.

Ashley Boettcher

"Far away there in sunshine are my highest aspirations. I may not reach them, but I can look up and see their beauty, believe in them and try to follow where they lead."

-Louisa May Alcott

The Book of Dreams

The Life Story of a Teenage Girl

Prologue

Imagine a world of reality, a world of practicality. Imagine having your heart as hollow as the moon on a cold winter's night, where the frost burning your face is like the flame that burns your dreams.

Where hopes you hold are dissolved and promises made for the future are left lurking in the darkest part of your soul.

In this world you learn to live for yourself, look out for "number one", and care for no one else, to forget prince Charming and the fantasy of the princess locked in the tower.

The ethics of this civilization causes us to choke back tears; block all feeling; forget all dreams.

Reality has stripped you down to nothing, and you have nothing left to give.

Morgan Parker found this world to be real and painful one summer night. It penetrates every fiber of a young woman's soul.

At an early age, after her father leaves and her grandmother dies, Morgan realizes she has no will to feel anymore. She is taught to extinguish the candles of her heart, close the door to her soul's inner chambers. Now she has no feelings, no thought, no will to even live. She believes, "I am only worth what I appear to be."

If a girl is black or if she is white; blonde or dark. She's stupid if she shares her mind. Undesirable if she bears her soul, and she is unattractive if she saves her innocence.

Morgan Parker becomes numb.

She must be desensitized to survive, in her eyes. She must be demoralized, disconnected, and deadened.

Morgan is left with the shattered glass of her past so commonly found in the lives of so many girls her age.

This once precious child is gone.

She has learned to grow up before her time, to put away the toys and the fiction, the romance and love.

For years her heart aches until she can't deny her souls forgotten dreams any longer.

She will find an answer to God's plan for her life and future, find out there is a happy ending, and fairy tales do come true.

Join Morgan Parker on this exciting and emotional adventure in unlocking her hearts bolted door, and discover the mystical world of a young woman who reaches for a higher goal within herself.

She can only find it deep within herself, here, in The Book of Dreams.

"What you do speaks so loudly
that I cannot hear what you say."
- *Ralph Waldo Emerson*

~ Chapter One ~

*Taken from "The Sisterhood of the Traveling Pants" by Ann Brashares.
Delacorte Press- an imprint of Random House Children's Books, a division of
Random House, Inc. Used with permission.*

~ Chapter One ~

Morgan Parker sat lonely in her bedroom staring at the lace that draped from her canopy. Her frail body was piled in a heap of silk from her nightgown and robe. Her tears seemed to cause everything in the room to bleed together and swirl around like a bowl of warm ice cream. She let a tear fall from her rounded cheek, and watched it run onto her soft velvet pillows. She laid back onto the piled lump of pillows, forcing the air in and out of her lungs seemed harder in this position. Morgan was still and somber picking at a loose thread in her embroidered blanket.

Looking around, she considered her soft pink walls, painted in vertical stripes, and the teddy bears neatly laid on a high shelf. Morgan sat up and wiped the salty tears off her face. The twelve year old tried to rationalize what she was hearing in the next room.

"Ok, they are angry, about what? Only God knows."

"They're talking it out…. yeah right. Ugh!"

"Stop it!"

She thought, clasping her hands over her ears to block out the screaming of her parents' argument. To make matters worse, her baby brother had been woken up by the noise, and now joined in.

"I just want to disappear."

Morgan wanted to dissolve, evaporate, just stop…. being. She tried to concentrate on going back to sleep, but the angry words consumed every crevice of her mind.

"I can't take this, I can't take it anymore!" On impulse, she alighted, as she ran down the hall, her nightgown trailed on the floor behind her. Her angelic face was stained with running tears that had dried, and was streaked with a stabbing pain of neglect. She couldn't believe what this had come to. Today at school, she had to explain to her friends that her parents weren't getting a divorce, they were just going through some hard times, but she was lying to herself.

She heard her father slam his fist on the bureau, and her mother scream some unintelligible swear word.

"They spend so much time arguing, they have no energy left to be normal." Passing her report card on the fridge, Morgan thought,

"It's their fault I got a D in math. If mom cared, I wouldn't have to worry about measuring up or possibly staying back!"

Passing the kitchen table and thrusting the back door open, she let the cool summer air whisk her worries away. Bursting through the doorway, her heart danced with the pure freedom silence brought.

"Peace at last!"

She soaked in the warm June air. She let the moonlight dance on her head, and she tumbled onto the ground. Feeling the breeze pick her hair up and tickle the back of her neck, she felt chills run down her spine and out her toes. Sighing, she thought, "I'll never fight with my husband, and he will always love me. I'll stay married!" Laying back, Morgan plucked a piece of grass and split it into a thousand pieces. The stars seemed to sparkle and whisper sweet and vexing words of far away dreams. Of happy times, she remembered long ago. They were gone now.

"Fine!" her mother fumed.

"And don't expect me to take care of that either" Morgan heard her dad say.

"I never expected you to do anything here!"

"Yes you did, yes you did, Sarah!" Morgan's father protested.

"Ya know what…. ok, ok, this is it Mitch, if you think you can take off and…." Morgan's forehead wrinkled as she concentrated on nothing.

"Shut up, stop fighting," she hissed aloud.

Then her concentration was broken by the sound of the screen door slamming, and the shout of some obscene words. Then to her horror, her father's pick-up truck started.

Morgan's heart pounded harder. She sat up to see, only to find he had left.

Never to return.

"Living never wore one out so much as the effort not to live."

-Anis Nin

~ Chapter Two ~

~ Chapter Two ~

Morgan sat up, startled. Sweat poured down her temples, saturating her soft brown curls. Why did she have to dream about that awful evening again? It was the third time this week! Her father never came back and her mother was forced to sell the house she fought so hard in court to keep. Mitch rarely paid child support, and it was never enough when he did. Many of Morgan's toys were sold at tag sales or given to her brother instead. Two years ago, she would have never thought she would be helping raise her brother, Adam, leave her school and be living in a musty New York City apartment; a big change from their rambling Connecticut estate. Her mom traded her job as a CEO for a computer software company for selling perfume at some stingy salon on 5th Avenue, obviously knowing that she forfeited her life, and her children's lives too.

Morgan relaxed and swung her legs around to the side of the bed. She looked up from her pale, thin legs in front of her and gazed at her new room. Her walls were white; her beloved toys that she hid from being taken were in a box on the floor. Already, or maybe it was still, her shelves were dusty. She contemplated whether the previous renter ever cleaned. Her book collection was disorganized and strewn. The collection consisted of little more than an astronomy book she never returned to the library, biographies, and about 20 Nancy Drew Mysteries. Then one of her favorites, National Velvet, was crammed between some books about British writers of the 19th Century. In the back was an old Bible with a thick sheen of dust on it. Her eyes lingered on her dresser, which had a votive candle that was never lit, and an old music box from her grandmother that she never cared to play. Morgan peeled back her sticky cotton sheets on her bed and climbed out.

"I need a drink, maybe I'll get some Coke." She tiptoed over to her closet, which contained some old shoes, slippers, a couple of church dresses, a blouse and a box of sweaters and jeans. She reached for her bathrobe and headed down the hall. Her satin pajama bottoms made a swooshing noise every time she took a step. Morgan silently took a glass from the cupboard and filled it to the brim. Standing at the window, Morgan stared at the full moon as she took a gulp of warm soda.

"Full moons make people crazy," she thought.

"Maybe I won't have to go to school because I've temporarily lost my mind. If I do go to school, maybe I'll get hit by a car before I get there, just maybe..." she toyed.

Morgan stared at her half-empty glass.

"I know I'm not going to like high school. Mia said junior high was worse; that doesn't relieve this stale, aching feeling I have." She dumped the fizzy mud down the drain and proceeded down the hall. Thinking of ways to avoid talking to other kids, Morgan's thoughts were interrupted by the soothing voice of her mother. She was singing a familiar but unknown lullaby Morgan recognized. She peered into little Adam's room. Her mother was bent over the three-year-olds' bed, tucking his arm under the sheets. Her nightgown made her look like an angel, and her hair was up in a bun that fell around the deep creases in her forehead. Strands curved into the lines she wore around her eyes.

"Morgan! It's almost one in the morning!
Go to bed!" her mother said with an annoyed tone.

"I was thirsty."

"Honey, you have school tomorrow, I don't want to have to pick you up from detention because you fell asleep or mouthed off in class because you're so tired, go to bed!" Morgan's mother boomed.

Adam stirred slightly.

"I'm sorry. I said I was thirsty," Morgan retorted with a tone of returned annoyance.

"Right now...."

Her mother's frustrated threat bore itself in the dark frown that fringed her mouth. Morgan knew to leave, but couldn't hold back the confused thoughts she had dammed back.

"Mom, why do I have to go anyway? I don't want to! Lots of kids don't graduate and are fine in life. I mean, I'll get married, and my husband will be smart and make money and stuff."

"Dear," her mother started, with sarcasm dripping from every syllable.

"Men marry so they can have a mommy to take care of them. Take my advice, don't get married at all. You'll only get heartbroken."

Morgan's heart raced.

The words she was thinking exploded in her head and bounced around in her mouth, threatening to expose themselves.

It was too late.

They did.

"I already am heartbroken, mom, thanks."

She turned and slammed the door. To her satisfaction, scaring Adam, making him cry.

"Why did I do that?" she regretfully thought.

"I can't do this, I'm spent. I just don't get it. My parents were so perfect together, and then, Bang! It was all gone. Now mom hates men, more and more, and says it all the time."

"Where are you God? Don't you care? How can you let this happen? Do you think this is funny?

We have been alone, depending on ourselves and you're just pretending not to see.

Answer me!"

She screamed in her head.

"Answer, please?....."

Morgan began to sob. Then she dozed off. Knowing this was the start of what would be a very bad day.

" It is terribly amusing how many different climates of feeling one can go through in one day."

-Anne Morrow Lindberge

~ Chapter Three ~

~ Chapter Three ~

Morgan's throat was dry. She felt like a ship taking on water. Guys from all around stared at every piece of her. She squirmed to think what they were saying to themselves. She compulsively pushed the bridge of her glasses up so they sat square between her eyes, making the nose pads squeeze tears out of the corners of her eyes.

She looked down as girls in mini-skirts past, staring at her low-rise jeans.

"So dorky," she thought

Then like a hurricane, some jerk plowed her into a locker.

"Sorry!" he beckoned as his arm slithered around some ugly girl.

"Snots," she said to herself.

In class, it was the same, if not a little better, but the staring, leering, the whispering, and antagonizing got worse by sixth period.

Luckily, as she was headed to her locker, she ran into Mia for the first time that day. Mia was her best friend from first grade to sixth grade. Then she moved to New York a few years before Morgan did, and now they had met up again.

"I can't take it Mia," she said to her Italian friend.

"Why? When you're pretty like me, you take it as a complement."

"I'm not pretty like you," Morgan retorted.

"Ok, so you're not, but believe me, that doesn't matter to these animals. They are at their worst in high school. Just watch out."

"For what?" Morgan asked stunned.

"For the guys, the popular ones. You may find some good Christians, but they are rare in this school. I wouldn't be surprised if we were the only ones...."

"You're considering me a 'Christian'?" Morgan thought.

"I wouldn't even, the only time I pray is when I am complaining of need something."

Morgan was shocked by her own honesty. She said good-bye to Mia and watched her walk away.

She was tall and thin, a perfect figure. She had an hourglass shape, which was accentuated by the pattern on her shirt and the word "Hotty." Her long black curls spun a web-like design across her shoulder blades and delicately bounced with every step.

She was the person Morgan wanted to be. Her own shape was more similar to a carrot, with the poofy leaves on top. Her hair always frizzed and had the mixed hair color that you couldn't even call "just brown." She looked like a mouse, but even mice had pretty eyes. That was the only redeemable aspect about herself, she thought.

Her hands were long and bony; her stature towered at a honking 5'2". To make matters worse, these stupid reading glasses that covered her pleasant eyes labeled her a 'geek.' People knew, like it was stamped on her head.

"Make fun of me, I have no confidence to destroy anyway."

"Hey," an unfamiliar voice beckoned.

"Oh, God, no," Morgan thought.

She turned around and planted a fake smile on her face.

"Hi."

"I'm Angela, Angela O'Toole, you're a freshman too?"

"Yeah, I am. I'm Morgan Parker."

"Hmm, well this is my locker." Angela gestured to her metal door.

Morgan observed Angela's locker was next to hers. She had already decorated it with posters and things that dangled. A picture of Jesus' face with thorns on his head was at eye level.

Then a tomb with a rock rolled away below that. Morgan got a glimpse of the writing on it, "When God Closes One Door, He Always Opens Another. Angela put her books neatly on the shelf.

In color order.

"Weird."

Morgan glanced at her own locker. Some old 'Limp Bizkit" sticker was still stuck on it, but chipped on the edges, and the print had worn away. Her books were thrown in a heap.

Some girls were gossiping in the corner behind them, and a gang-banger was harassing another girl. Morgan tried to turn away, but Angela started talking again.

"I saw you in three of my classes. We should sit next to each other!"

"Yeah, sure."

Morgan diverted her eyes from the mouth full of metal in front of her, smiling. Her dark skin accentuated the metallic glitter.

"Well, I'll, um, see you tomorrow, bye."

Morgan nodded and gave a wry smile and watched Angela, and

her unnaturally red hair, hurry out the door.

"Great, another person I wish I could be like, and I know I can't."

"Life is the first gift, love is the second, understanding the third."
-Marge Piercy

~ Chapter Four ~

~ Chapter Four ~

Afew weeks passed without incident. Morgan met a really nice South African kid named Ryan. He was on the honor roll, another thing she wanted, but wasn't smart enough to have. Angela became a good friend to Morgan, and Mia got along with her, too. They had a common interest in excessive body piercing. So things seemed to be settling down. What could possibly happen? Sophomore year in high school would be fine; turning 15 wouldn't be bad. Her brother wasn't old enough to be antagonizing her yet, and her mother was busy at work all the time

Stepping off the bus, Morgan eyed all directions for danger, and then proceeded down the sidewalk after waving to Ryan, who got off at the next stop. Pigeons wobbled around at her feet and trash blew past her ankles.

Morgan climbed the front steps of her building and raced up the four flights of stairs.

"Apartment AA23," she thought.

"Hmm, that's the detention block Princess Leah was in before she was rescued."

Morgan forgot about herself being rescued
long ago.

Her father couldn't even stick around.

What guy would want to come into her life and try to fix it?

Who would want someone would didn't cook, clean, or pray right, anyway? God didn't. That was evident to her.

She unlocked the door, thrust her backpack on the kitchen chair, and rounded the corner to see her mother on the living room couch.... with a man! Morgan took a step back. When did this happen?

"Honey, this is Jared."

"Uh, ok," she muttered, eyes bulging.

Jared gave her a warm smile. Or was it? He seemed to posses an unhealthy look of perversion. His skin oozed with a hunger for sex.

Morgan's stomach churned.

Her mother touched his hand and said, "We are seeing each other Morgan, we've been going out."

Morgan's head began to spin. Her arms hung limply at her side and she detected the sensation of drool threatening to spill out of her mouth.

She stood up and closed her mouth, trying to look intelligent.

"We are going out tonight. Could you watch Adam for me? He's up from his nap now."

Since when did she care how long he napped? Or even bother to monitor him in his room.

"We will be leaving at five, ok?"

"Ok."

Morgan slumped and turned away.

"Nice to meet you, Meagan," Jared called.

Morgan flinched, but kept on until she got to her room. There she proceeded to bury her face in a pillow and scream until her lungs felt like they could collapse. Maybe she was wrong; things were getting worse.

She counted until 9:00 p.m., and put Adam to bed. Ten, eleven. Still not back. Maybe they went dancing…. or not. Morgan decided not to stay up anymore. She locked and dead bolted the door. She turned off the lights and went to bed.

Light streamed in Morgan's window. She hadn't pulled down the blinds, but that was no longer an issue. She heard talking in the kitchen. She got up, raked her hair with her fingers, and thumped down the hall. What she saw, she didn't like.

Jared.

"What is love? Love is chance, a sudden glance, a poet's lance, a dreamers dance."

-Anonymous

~ Chapter Five ~

Happy Endings Produced by Christine Staudiger
Woman's Day Magazine
February 11th 2003 66th year 5th issue page 162

~ Chapter Five ~

"Good morning!" Jared said cheerfully.
"Right, for you maybe."

"Morgan!" her mother sassed, slamming her plate of toast. Adam eyed Jared suspiciously. Morgan had no need to. She couldn't even look at him. She knew what happened. Regardless of how far it went, it did, and she hated him for it.

"Off to school, huh?" Jared started.

"Yeah, wish you would too."

"Morgan Ann!" Morgan's mother bellowed.

"May I see you for a minute!?"

"No, I have to get ready for school... or throw up," Morgan muttered and raced down the hall before she was cornered.

She never did this.

This wasn't normal.

Because the situation wasn't normal.

Nothing was 'normal' anymore.

"Angela, my mom is dating a total creep!"

"How do you know?" Angela probed. Her red pigtails bounced from the bus hitting a pothole.

"He just is, I can tell."

Angela nodded understandingly while Mia gave Morgan a skeptical look.

"Ok...." and she returned to her Walkman.

"Ya know," Ryan turned around from the seat in front of them.

"We should actually find out. I mean, what if this dude has a police record or something?!" His accent articulated police.

Angela and Morgan turned and looked at each other questionably.

"Or we can go beat him up," Ryan suggested trying to flex his muscles.

Mia gave an involuntary snort.

"Not needed," Morgan replied.

"Even if he could!" Mia called across the aisle.

"I know he's just a creep," Morgan finished.

"Is you're mom saved?" Angela questioned.

"Is she what? "Morgan returned.

"Saved, accepted Christ…. believes in the resurrection, sins-gone… bye-bye?"

"Uh, no, er, I don't know, maybe?"

"How come you always say that?" Ryan asked.

"Say what?"

"Maybe," Ryan replied.

"Well, I'm not sure of a lot of stuff, I guess I just doubt a lot, heck, sometimes I doubt myself."

Ryan turned around and ignored Morgan.

What she really wanted was for someone to notice her pain; to get her help, to know what she needed. To hold her and say, "It's ok now."; to come and rescue the princess, and be carried off into the sunset.

That wouldn't happen.

Would she have to say it to get some attention around here?

Or did she have to convert into the bimbos running around the halls at school?

That was something she didn't want, and yes, couldn't have.

Even if she did want it.

"Of the thirty-six ways of avoiding disaster, running away is best."

-*Anonymous*

~ Chapter Six ~

~ Chapter Six ~

"Hey dumpling!" Morgan's grandmother called.
Today was her 15th birthday. There was only three weeks of summer left, so the party was out on the sunny roof. Everyone was here.

Mom, Adam, Mia, and Angela. Even Ryan. Grandpa, Grammy....

Jared, with a big stupid grin on his face.

Morgan's party guests sang the birthday song and everyone clapped as Morgan blew out her candles.

While eating, Morgan watched everyone. Adam was winding Jared up in party streamers, and Grammy was looking at her, smiling.

"What did you wish for?"

"If I told you, it wouldn't come true."

Morgan's grandmother laughed and gave her a wink.

Just then, Morgan's mom stood up.

"Everyone, I have an announcement!"

Morgan rolled her eyes, secretly.

"Jared and I, well we have been dating since.... well, forever, and...."

Morgan's breathing became shallow. Everyone seemed to move in slow motion. The images in front of her distorted and blurred.

She knew what was coming.

"What Sarah is trying to say is, well, we are getting married in May!"

Jared made a cheers gesture and kissed Morgan's mom.

Everyone was laughing and talking about the news, but Morgan was in complete shock. No, she was past shock, disbelief, denial, or even refusal.

Down right dismissal.

No reaction was coming out; she was frozen in her chair.

"Morgan, honey, isn't it wonderful?"

Morgan looked up.

"Yes mother."

Her mom looked shocked. She never called her 'mother,' but she dismissed Morgan's strongly pathetic reply. What Morgan really wanted to say was, "Oh yes, what was it you said last year? Ahh, it was: 'Don't get married, you'll only get heartbroken.' Isn't that right?"

Seems she couldn't bear to hurt her mother. She was laughing and smiling.

She hadn't been this happy in six or seven years!

Somehow, it seemed cheap.

Now everything seemed cheap. Even her chair, the air she breathed, the ground she walked on was worth nothing. She let her fork slide out of her hand.

Now she felt cheap.

She was like a prisoner in her own body, unable to move or speak.

She felt stupid.

Her birthday celebration had become an engagement party instead. She slunk off without even opening her presents. No one noticed, they were too busy talking to Jared and the oh-so sappy bride-to-be.

Happy birthday Morgan Parker! Everyone loves you so much!

While Morgan sulked on her bed, Mia walked in.

"What's wrong, Morgan?"

"I don't like him, I never have, Mia, how am I going to deal with this maturely?"

"You are just going to have to pray a lot."

Morgan snorted.

"Ohmigod, I cannot believe you Morgan!"

"What?! Morgan shrieked.

"Not all of us are all perfect like you. You're so pious!"

"Pious?" Mia questioned.

"You need to get serious about your life and where it's going." Mia confronted her.

"Why are you changing this?! This isn't about me!" Morgan replied.

"It isn't?"

Mia calmly got up and left.

"She's right," a half Ryan-Mom voice told her.

"You're so selfish, your own mother is getting married and you're jealous because she interrupted cake time."

Morgan lowered her head and blushed with embarrassment.

"You couldn't sink any lower Morgan," she told herself.

"Now I can't go back out. It will be too awkward."

She picked at a hangnail on her thumb.

"But if I stay, I'll get in trouble for being a total snot!"

"I'll say I felt sick."

"Great, now you're lying," her conscience scolded.

"You turned out to be a great girl."

Morgan just wanted to curl up and die. One, because of what life was like; two, because of what she was like.

"Morgan!" mom called.

Morgan's heart sank. She was in for it. Walking out onto the roof, she saw her grandparents rising.

"Morgan, say thank-you and good-bye," her mother told her curtly.

Morgan held her breath as she bid them good-bye, and her friends left. Mia gave Morgan a weary look.

"Morgan Ann Parker!" her mother began as the door closed.

"How dare you do this!? How rude can you possibly be? You are unbelievable!"

"I just didn't know what to say," Morgan defended herself timidly.

"Your mother and I know this is hard for you…." Morgan flashed Jared a warning look.

"Why are you attacking me, Morgan?!" her mother asked.

"No, why are you attacking me?!" Morgan reversed the question hoping to take the heat off of herself.

"You are such a brat," her mother stated.

Morgan felt a flood of emotion.

"How dare she," Morgan thought.

"I hate you."

She flew down the stairs, kept running, and didn't stop when she reached the street.

Morgan felt as if her feet weren't even touching the ground. She didn't bother running on the sidewalk. Brooklyn pedestrian traffic was building up. She raced between a parking meter and flew past cars stopped at a light.

A cab beeped at her.

Finally, after what felt like four blocks, Morgan stopped. Stock-still.

"Why? What is this for? Why am I even living?"

Morgan almost fell flat when she felt the bumper of a car and a loud horn.

"Hey you! Stupid! Get out of the road," the angry driver shouted.

Morgan trudged onto the sidewalk and laid down on the cold pavement. A business woman in a suit walked past the heaving girl, and stared at her, confused.

It was after 7:00 p.m., and it was getting dark, but New York was lighting up.

What risk would she take? Go home and get pummeled? Or stay out for a night on the town.

She decided to decide in the morning.

"Part of the trouble is, I've never properly understood that some disasters accumulate, that they don't all land like a child out of an apple tree."

- Janet Borroway

~ Chapter Seven ~

~ Chapter Seven ~

It was about 1:00 am when Morgan finally gave up. It was too cold to stand around, too scary to be so vulnerable, and she was really tired. Morgan knew her building should be locked- and she didn't have a key, to anything. She stopped short at the door, realizing her mistake.

"Stupid, stupid, stupid!" she said, stomping her foot.

Morgan started shivering and chills ran down her spine from the cold, or was it from the awful idea she had?

"There is a key to the apartment on the roof.... and the roof door had no lock...."

It was dangerous, but possible!

Rising, Morgan's heart beat faster and her stomach ached. The 15 year old walked down the alley on the side of her apartment building, and trotted up to a dumpster.

It was just like a movie!

The fire escape ladder was right there.

"A box, a box, I need a box or something."

Morgan grabbed a TV box out of the dumpster and stood on it to shut the lid.

Then she cautiously rose on top of the dumpster and lowered the retractable ladder. The rust caused the metal stairway to grind and screech the more it moved.

It was so loud she stopped.

"What if the people on the second floor hear? They will either call the police or my mom!"

Morgan tested the ladder.

It would stay still if she didn't pull too hard; if she could jump onto one of the rungs and climb from there it wouldn't make as much noise!

"Too many 'ifs' to make this mission turn out successful," she thought.

Morgan considered her other options.

"There are none,"

She thought, wiping sweat off her nose.

She stepped to the far edge of the dumpster and took a running leap.

She jumped and caught the 6th rung up, but she was too heavy, and the ladder slid down!

She bounced off and hit her nose on the bottom rung. Blood splattered everywhere. She violently fell on the dumpster and rolled to the pavement below.

Morgan didn't know how long she was out, but what she did know was that she was freezing, and wet. Her face was dripping and muddy. Something sticky covered her hands and neck, but even in the dark, she could tell what it was. Then she tasted metal in her mouth. In disgust, she spit a wad of blood on the ground.

Her face, arms, hands, and clothes had blood on them, from her broken nose. Pain pounded every part of her body.

Morgan was shaking from fright, and from the sight of so much blood. She sat up and saw she had ripped a hunk of skin off her wrist, and it was bleeding profusely.

Morgan had no watch but figured it was probably 2:00 am by now, and it was getting colder.

"There is no way in, and I'm not going to call her from a pay phone to let me in, I could go to the hospital though." Then realizing she had no money, she thought, "I can make it, I'll just be real careful."

Surveying her condition as a car past, Morgan decided to climb again.

She ascended much more cautiously this time. Since the ladder was down, she stepped on it and slowly went up.

"15, 16, 17…." She counted the whole way up.

At the top, she found a chair and sat down. Her whole body was shaking.

"Get it together! Get the key; unlock the door and go to sleep. The hard part is over."

Morgan got up and went to the doorframe.

She felt around, under the mat, in the flowerpots, chairs, tables-her search covered the entire roof. No key found.

"Now what?!" she shouted.

"Are you trying to kill me? What about it God? You hate me, don't you?"

Morgan looked up at the sky laughing and crying hysterically. She collapsed on the cement and thought about her options again.

"I could go into the hall and wait for mom to open the door, or sleep up here until she goes to work. Either way, this sucks!"

Finding a beach chair, Morgan curled up and went to sleep.

"There is nothing like returning to a place that remains unchanged to find the ways in which you yourself have altered."

-Nelson Mandela

~ Chapter Eight ~

~ Chapter Eight ~

Noisy streets flooded Morgan's ears. She tried to lift her head, but she couldn't tell if it was a sore neck or dried blood gluing her to the seat cushion. Ripping her head off the vinyl, she noticed it was the latter, but her muscles were sore. She got up and walked over to the wall. There was an accident below. A digital clock read, "52 degrees… 7:02 am."

"Mom is probably leaving now."

Morgan strode to the door, yanked it open, and went around the corner to her apartment door.

"Thank God, the door is unlocked!"

The praise was short lived. Apparently, she mis-timed her mothers' departure. All three people standing in the kitchen ceased what they were doing and stood still, staring.

Morgan looked down.

Her pink tee shirt had black-crusted blood, and she was all scuffed up. Her hair obviously had blood in it and her face felt clogged with splattered mud.

"Oh my God, Morgan, what happened?!"

"You look like you got hit by a car," Jared chuckled.

"Jared, I told you to get out," her mother screamed.

Morgan's mom pulled up a chair as Morgan stood in shock.

What in the world happened while she was gone?

Jared fled the scene while Morgan's mom got ice and stuck it on her eye.

"Did someone do this to you?" She sobbed.

"I…. um,"

Morgan cleared her throat.

"I fell, off a, um…. dumpster."

Morgan's mom blinked.

"Trying to get inside."

"Oh hon! It's ok now."

Adam sucked on his juice cup, bewildered.

"What happened to Morgie?"

"She fell and got a boo-boo, Adam," Morgan answered.

"Mom, I'm ok now, I just need a shower, ok? Just leave me alone now."

Morgan's mother stopped peeling the backing off a band-aid and stepped back, understandingly.

"Ok, but come right back out, you might need stitches."

"What?!" Morgan asked in shock.

She jogged down the hall and spun into the bathroom. There it was, an awful, deep slice across her lip, up to her bloody nose. Her left eye was purple and protruding, and her ear was grotesquely coated in blood from her mangled hairline.

"I do look like I got mugged," she thought.

"Call me if you need anything!"

"Don't you have work?"

"I am taking the day off," she said quietly.

"Why?" Morgan asked cautiously.

There was a long pause, then Morgan turned to find her mother standing in the bathroom doorway. Morgan noted she was in sweats. She never looked like a bum unless something was wrong.

"Jared and I aren't getting married anymore."

"It's my fault, isn't it?" Morgan half asked, half apologized.

"No, I should thank you…. For helping me realize what a jerk he is. He would never support us, Morgan. He's just like your father. We had a big fight, and well, he accidentally revealed his true self."

Her mom wiped away a tear.

"Hmm, first time in the six months we have been together," her mom said in a tense high voice, obviously fighting back a flood of emotion. She just looked down and shrugged.

Then she started crying. Big round tears rolled down her sandpapery skin, dropping onto the shag carpet.

"I'm sorry, it is my fault, and I was selfish yesterday."

Morgan's throat was closing up as she fought back her own tears. Her face grew warn as she continued.

"I'm sorry about what I said," she stated vaguely.

"Honey, it's all ok now, things will be back to the way they were, soon."

Relieved, Morgan took her shower and after, laid down and went to sleep.

"Friends listen to what you say, best friends listen to what you don't say."

-Tim McGraw

~ Chapter Nine ~

Wise Words "The Gift of Friendship" Produced by Christine Staudinger Woman's Day Magazine April 1st 2003 66th year 7th issue Page 148 Chapter Nine

~ Chapter Nine ~

Morgan's alarm went off at 5:45 am, Monday morning. It had been three weeks since her accident, and all evidence of her fall was gone, except the scar on her top lip. It was her sophomore year. School went by so quickly last year, she thought time would punish her by making this school year agonizingly slow. Morgan walked down her school hall and met up with Ryan and Mia.

"Hey guys," Mia greeted.

"Hmm," Morgan grunted.

"I've got news," Ryan began.

"My friend from South Africa might be coming over our senior year as an exchange student!"

"That's great," Mia praised.

Morgan collected her books and headed to class. Angela took her seat next to Morgan.

Morgan looked around.

Most of the people in her class were like Ryan or Angela. Morgan didn't see many white kids at this school.

Until she looked up.

She never really noted who sat in front of her.

It was a guy; he looked tall, athletic, and seemed popular.

He wore his hair in short spikes with blonde tips. He was joking about something to his buddies.

Morgan beckoned to Angela.

Angela spun around to address Morgan. Her pinkish hair whipped over her eyes.

"What?"

"Who is that?" Morgan pointed to the chair directly in front of her.

"Oh, that's Mike Miganouski."

"Hmm."

"Beware, Morgan."

Morgan turned around to take a second look; he was turned sideways at his desk so she could see his profile.

"He's cute," she commented.

"Yeah, but dangerous. He's always after vulnerable girls. People say he's a real womanizer," Angela whispered.

Morgan turned back into her seat. She listened to him when he answered questions in class.

"So smart," she thought.

She listened to the way he talked, and thought, "He's so cool."

When class ended, she even watched how he walked.

"Nice."

"Huh?" Mia questioned.

"Did I say that out loud?"

"Um, yeah?!"

"Oops."

"Who's nice? Let me see!" Mia played.

"He's gone now," Morgan said sadly.

"Aww! Darn!" Mia toyed.

"His name is Mike Miganouski."

"Huh, I hear he's really good in biology, maybe you could ask him to tutor you."

Morgan thought a little...

"Angela said he's a creep."

"Yeah, that's true, but people only say that, you never know," Mia offered.

"Oh, I'd be too scared to ask him out!"

"No, no, you don't have to; have him tutor you to see if he's nice, if he isn't, say you don't want to take lessons anymore. If he is nice, he'd catch on, and ask you out!"

"You are wise, master yoda!" Morgan teased, and the two walked home together.

The next day, Morgan couldn't keep her eyes off of Mike, and the next, and the next. Even until Friday, she watched his every move.

Morgan stared after him as he took a drink at the water fountain.

"Hey Angela," Mia said.

"Lookie, I got a new hole!" Angela pointed to the fourth ring in her upper earlobe.

Mia fingered her large hoops.

"Yeah, I've been wanting to get a third hole, what do you think, Morgan?"

Morgan paid no attention.

"Morgan.... earth to Morgan!"

"What?"

"What is with you?" Angela questioned.

"Mike Miganouski."

"Oh Morgan, stop it."

"Stop what?"

"Gawking," Angela stated.

"Why, isn't he cute?"

"I don't stare at guys."

Mia gave Morgan a warning look like, "don't go there." But she did.

"Don't tell me you don't date!"

"I don't."

Morgan stood shocked.

"You're 16 years old and you don't date?!"

"It's my choice. I just don't think I should be looking for a mate when I'm not ready to get married."

"Ok...." Morgan turned slowly and slammed her locker shut.

It was different, not dating, but she couldn't afford not to, she had to prove she fit in just as well as the rest, and she was willing to do anything for it.

At lunch, Morgan directed her friends to sit across from the jock table.

"This is too close," Ryan commented.

"I should not be here, we should not be here."

Mia stared at the yellow goop on her tray.

"What do you see? I see maggots," she stated.

"No, I see melted make-up," Angela said.

"I think it looks like over cooked rice," Ryan added.

"That's what it is, moron!"

Morgan jokingly threw her spoon at him, drawing the attention of Mike.

He stared at her for a while, then got up as his companions whispered to him.

Morgan's face felt hot, she knew it was red. Her heart pounded harder as he knelt at her seat.

"Hello, ladies!" He directly spoke to Ryan in a mocking tone.

"I don't believe we've met...." he added, looking at Morgan.

"I'm Meagan, er, Morgan, Morgan Parker."

"I heard from a reliable source you were looking for a tutor."

He rose from his stooped position and slid a napkin with a phone number on it, across the table.

Morgan sat, starring at the napkin as he walked away.

All of Mike's buddies cheered him on.

"Bye?" she said belatedly.

Ryan stifled a laugh.

"What? Quit laughing, you're just jealous cause you don't have a boyfriend."

"Hey!" Ryan defended himself.

"I told you to steer clear, this is your chance, Morgan," Angela warned.

"No way!"

"Fine, it's your funeral!" Angela clashed her tray into a garbage can behind Morgan and left.

Mia and Ryan carried on their conversation while Morgan was left, alone, staring at the napkin.

"You will do foolish things, but do them with enthusiasm! "

-Colette, French writer

~ Chapter Ten ~

~ Chapter Ten ~

Morgan's hands were sweaty and pale. She was shaking as she dialed the numbers 577…4.

She hung up.

Should she actually call a boy?

She was startled by the phone in her hands ringing.

Morgan screamed and teetered in her chair then thumped onto the floor.

She crawled over and pushed the 'on' button.

"Hello?" she said slowly.

"Yo, this is Mike, this Morgan?"

"Yeah."

"Cool, cool, so yo, how's it goin', in school and stuff?"

Morgan thought. Should she be honest?

"Ok! Actually, I do need help in Spanish."

"Well, I'm down with that. What do ya say we go have a couple of shakes and look over the books?"

"Ok," Morgan said calmly, but she was screaming inside.

"How about tonight?"

Morgan answered before he even finished his question.

"Yeah, that's great."

"How about 8?"

Morgan's heart sank. Her mom would be home and wouldn't want to watch Adam for her.

"Um, my mom will be home then."

"Ok, later?" he questioned.

Morgan's heart jumped. Later? Like sneaking-out-later? It was dangerous, and Morgan liked the idea.

"Yeah, later, like 10:00."

"I'm down," he said.

"So I presume this is a date?"

It was silent.

Morgan slammed her head on the cupboard for opening her mouth.

"Yeah, yeah it is."

"What?! did he say yes?!" she questioned.

"Ok, see you then."

She slowly put down the receiver and sat still for a second.

Then she squealed and spread out on the floor like she was making a snow angel. She ran to her room and found a pair of jeans to go with her blouse.

She looked at the clock.

6:19 it read.

Her mom should be home really soon.

Just then, she heard the door.

"Hey mom," she said, going over to greet her.

"Hmm," her mother mumbled.

She threw herself on the couch and turned on the evening news.

Morgan ran into her brother's room.

Adam was crashing two soldiers together in fierce combat.

"Ok Adam, time to clean up, time to get ready for bed.

"Nooooo," he whined.

Morgan snatched the warriors from his tiny fists and threw them in a box full of toys.

Adam screeched in disapproval.

"Adam, stop it, you need to clean up."

Adam shot a toy block at her.

"Adam, pick that up right now."

"No."

"Now."

"No."

"Adam!" Morgan bellowed, frustrated.

She heard her mother call to her from the living room couch.

"Morgan, don't yell at him."

"Easy for you to say," she thought.

She put Adam in his pj's and picked up the toys and monitored him while he brushed his teeth.

She glanced down the hall to the kitchen clock.

"8:10... just enough time."

She observed her mom at the couch in the adjacent room watching Seinfeld and eating out of a carton of ice cream.

"She is still going to be up!" she thought horrified.

Morgan plunked Adam into his bed and turned off the lights.

"Morgie!" Adam sobbed.

"Don't you dare get out of that bed!" Morgan threatened.

She noticed her mom had turned off the TV and went to the bathroom.

Morgan raced into her room and quietly shut the door. She changed and put on some lip-gloss.

She inserted a gold stud earring into each ear and added small hoops in the bottom holes.

Then her mom's bedroom door shut.

It was 8:29 pm.

"Why am I rushing? I have over an hour!"

Morgan flopped onto her bed and waited.

Everything was quiet. Too quiet.

She rose and crept to her door, peered out and found the light that usually streamed under her mother's door was extinguished.

She went out and shut the door behind her.

There was a huge crash as Morgan ran into a toy truck on the dark hallway floor.

She cringed silently for a few seconds, then moved on to the kitchen.

She opened the door and silently shut it after she exited.

Morgan flew up the corridor and out onto the roof.

She glanced at her watch in the moonlight.

"It's 9:15- I'll have plenty of time to get down there," she thought.

Morgan proceeded down the escape ladder and bounced down onto the street below. She looked around for any cars or people.

It was clear.

She rounded the alley onto the main road and sat at the steps to her building. She had an awful nauseating feeling in her gut. Guilt.

"This is a bad idea Morgan, go back in!" Mia's voice echoed in her head.

Then a car pulled up, it was too late to turn back now. So she shut Mia's voice out of her head and jumped in the car.

"I'm as pure as the driven slush."
- Tallulah Bankhead

~ Chapter Eleven ~

~ Chapter Eleven ~

"So…" Mike slurred as he parked the car outside a convenience store.

"So… what?" Morgan sarcastically replied.

"Wanna make out?"

Morgan was stunned.

"No!" She shrieked.

"I cannot believe I snuck out of my room to be with a guy who only wants to make out in a car in front of a dairy mart."

"I guess you aren't the girl I thought you were," Mike said manipulatively.

Morgan sat still, shocked.

"What is that supposed to mean?"

"All the guys were saying what a hottie you are and stuff. I guess you're not."

"What does that have to do with anything?!" Morgan questioned, annoyed.

"Well, if you're such a hottie, how come you won't make out with me?"

Morgan was losing. Was it true? She wasn't a dork. People really did think she was cool. She didn't want to lose that image.

"Um, ok, I just don't go around giving myself away!"

"Well, that is what you're supposed to do, guys like that."

Morgan felt a pounding in her entire body. She was on the edge. Butterflies were in her stomach. She needed to make a very important decision.

"So either you're hot or you're not," Mike interrupted.

"Ok, fine." Morgan gave in.

Mike leaned over her in the dark car.

Morgan let her emotions drive her.

Mike's hands traveled places they shouldn't have, but Morgan shut out the screams in her head of "this is wrong."

This was her chance to fit in, Mike was popular, she was not. If he went back with a good report, all was fine. So she let him do what he wanted, until she caught sight of the time on her watch, which was illuminated by the parking lot lamp outside.

It was 10:40, and for some strange, but legitimate reason, she couldn't do this anymore. It was too late to keep herself from doing something wrong, but she could prevent further mistake.

"Mike, I can't do this anymore."

"Oh come on babe," Mike whined.

"He sounds like my little brother…. eww!"

Morgan ripped Mike off of her, making him slam into the driver side window.

"What is wrong with you?" he yelled.

"I am just… anxious, that my mom will find out!" she lied.

"Cool, cool, I get 'cha."

"Could you drive me home?"

"Ok," Mike murmured.

"But let's do this again sometime."

"Ok."

Morgan clasped her hands on her mouth.

She just said 'ok'.

"What is wrong with me?? No, not ok."

Then a voice popped into her head.

"Either you're hot or you're not. Be what people think you are. You will become that attractive person."

The voice slithered around in her head and rested there satisfied. She liked the idea.

"How about a date next Friday?"

"That's cool," Mike replied.

Morgan felt a satisfied grin on her face, then in horror realized it was the same grin Jared always wore.

She was perverted, dirty; wrong.

The 15 year old was torn between what she wanted and what was right.

A voice told her to keep the date and call Mia for advice.

Morgan got out of the car and walked up to the building. She breathed in the crisp October air.

"Was that what I wanted?" she questioned.

"Is this an illusion of happiness, or is this how happiness works?"

"Some things have to be believed to be seen."

- Ralph Hodgson

~ Chapter Twelve ~

~ Chapter Twelve ~

"Hello?"

"Hey, Mia, I need your help."

"I'm here."

"Well, I went out with Mike last night, and I don't know what to do …"

There was a long silence as Mia waited for Morgan to continue.

"We went in a parking lot and made out."

"Morgan?! Why?" Mia asked, shocked.

"I don't know," Morgan agonized.

"I know I shouldn't have, but he convinced me it was good, ok…. right."

"Talk about role reversal in the Garden of Eden," Mia joked.

Morgan huffed.

"I made a date for next week, I mean, this Friday night, what should I do?"

"Hmm…." Mia thought.

"Maybe you should make a double date to clarify that it will NEVER happen again!

Morgan, normal people don't even kiss on their first dates, let alone going into a dark parking lot with a kid they don't even know!"

"I know, but this voice keeps telling me I'll add up to nothing without him."

"That's a lie, Morgan."

"I know it sounds stupid, but I want a boyfriend. I need one!"

"You don't need anyone to justify your existence, you should know that."

Morgan squirmed in her chair. Who should she listen to, the reliable voice on the other end of the receiver, or the voice bellowing in her head?

"Thanks, gotta go, Mia."

"Call me later this week!"

"Ok, bye."

Morgan's thoughts wandered for miles before coming back to the starting point.

She collected herself and decided to tell him no more after this, they weren't 'official' yet.

"Mike, you da man!" a guy called from down the hall.

Morgan felt very special and important.

Mike slung his arm around her shoulder and let his wrist bend so his hand hung down in front of her chest.

"Hey Morgan, great find…" a girl in the bathroom said.

"Thanks," she said sheepishly.

Now she couldn't say no. This happened all week. Thursday afternoon, Mike was fascinated with the skirt Morgan wore and led her out to his car during lunch. She didn't refuse.

Friday afternoon, Morgan invited Mike over to help her with her Spanish homework, then they would go out after.

"Morgan, the door!" her mother screamed.

Morgan wore a plain ribbed turtleneck and jeans. Her hair was up in a bun, but it had fallen out since Adam threw juice all over her shirt.

"Hey."

"Yo!" Mike said, inviting himself in.

"Dude, Mrs. P, how's it hangin'?"

"Morgan, who is this?" her mother questioned.

"A guy friend from school."

Then Morgan collected her courage.

"Mom, we're going out tonight."

Morgan squirmed in suspense.

"Morgan Ann Parker! Since when could you go getting boys without my permission?"

Morgan felt her stomach drop.

"Mom!" Morgan yelled embarrassed.

"I don't care, Morgan. I'd do this no matter who was standing there. You will not be going out with him tonight."

Mike took a leery step back. Morgan rolled her eyes and left the room.

"So where's your room?" Mike asked.

"Down there," Morgan pointed in the air throwing herself in the couch.

"Can I see it?"

"No!" Morgan squealed.

Mike looked down trying to look busy.

Then Morgan's mom came in.

"Morgan, why aren't you watching Adam?!"

"'Cause I'm doing my homework!"

"Don't get snotty!" her mom retorted.

"Bring him out here; I don't want to see him out of your sight when I get back!"

"Where are you going?"

"I am filling Joyce's shift, so I'll have a longer day."

Adam sauntered out of his room and happily sat on the scratchy rug in the living room with his blocks.

"Morgie, can you help?"

"Aww…" Mike said and slunk to the floor. Morgan tossed her pencil and threw her arms in the air.

A few minutes later, they got back to the homework.

"Ola, señorita," Mike began.

Morgan returned the greeting.

"So, ok, this is a conjunction, so…."

Morgan spaced out. How could she understand that? It made absolutely no sense to learn a language she didn't need.

"Morgan?"

"Huh?"

"Sooo, need a break, huh?"

Mike slid closer to Morgan. She realized Adam had fallen asleep on the floor.

"I have to go put him in his bed," Morgan announced, and released herself.

When she came back, Mike had taken off his shoes.

She plopped down and Mike slowly leaned over on top of Morgan.

Her mind raced.

She thought, "Not now, this is wrong."

The next thing she knew, they were laying down entangled on the couch when Morgan's mom came home.

Morgan's mother came into the room and screamed.

Mike jumped into the air like a cat that had cold water dumped on it.

Morgan sat up, realizing, some how, Mike had unbuttoned her pants. In horror, she zipped them up and chased down the hall after her mother.

"Mom, this isn't what it looks like."

Morgan slapped her forehead with the palm of her hand.

"What I mean, ok, so it is what it looks like, but really, that's all that it was."

Morgan's mom was standing in the bathroom doorway with her back turned. Her shoulders started bouncing and Morgan could hear her sniffling.

She looked over at Mike and gestured for him to leave. He grabbed his books and fled- in his stocking feet.

Morgan stood behind her mother patiently, expecting the worst, but she didn't do anything.

"I can't believe this. I thought I taught you better than this."

Morgan wavered, then gripped the wall for balance.

"All boys do is get you in trouble, Morgan, please don't do this, please."

Morgan knew she was right, she knew what to do.

"You're right; I'm going to break up with him."

"How you feel inside and how it reflects in your eyes is not something physical. "

- Sophia Loren

~ Chapter Thirteen ~

~ Chapter Thirteen ~

Her tears were more than she could handle. She wasn't in love; she wasn't even feeling like she was connected to him. There was just something traumatic about breaking up.

Morgan's eyes burned with regret and her mind was racing through thought after thought:

"I'll never fight with my husband, he will always love me."

"Honey, men marry so they can have a mommy to take care of them…"

"Either you're hot or you're not."

Morgan scrunched in a ball and tried to squeeze out the awful memories.

"This is it, Mitch!"

"My husband will be smart and make money…"

Morgan remembered her mother's best advice she ignored. She was so ignorant for letting her stupidity get in the way of her logic.

"You'll only get heartbroken."

"All boys do is get you in trouble…"

Her agony was interrupted by her mother's soft knock on the door.

"Honey, you need to get ready for school, you'll be late."

"Mom, I don't want to go."

"You'll prove he didn't have any affect on you if you go, looking fine," her mom coaxed.

A voice in Morgan's mind mocked, "He certainly had an affect on your pants!"

"Fine!" Morgan threw her limp body into a pair of jeans and put on her sneakers.

She grabbed her coat and her mom shoved gloves in her pocket and handed her a hat.

Morgan walked down the salted sidewalk to the bus stop. She knew she didn't look 'normal', and he would be satisfied to see she couldn't let this go easily.

"I hate my life," Morgan murmured, as she stared out the foggy window watching the yellow dotted lines whiz by.

Morgan stepped off the bus and watched the steam dissipate from her breath. Ice covered the sidewalk, like it covered her eyes, like it covered her heart, sending it into spasms. She was in a habitual brain-freeze.

Then a girl on the front stairs looked at Morgan and started whispering to her companion. Then another, and another. When she opened the doors and walked through the metal detector, there was a swarm of people looking at her- laughing. Morgan felt like she was going to fall over. Her head spun around her body. She felt like she was on a carousel horse. Her stomach was killing her. But she kept on walking. Her pants rubbed together and her shoes squeaked awkwardly on the shiny linoleum.

She fidgeted with her hair self-consciously.

Then she saw Mike.

Morgan had a feeling this would happen, but it didn't dull the shock.

There he was, with Laura Sheen hanging on his arm.

First Morgan felt pain, then nausea. It changed to rage as she grew closer to the couple. Then as she passed him, it changed to defiance. Suddenly she felt an emotion she never had before- vengeance.

Morgan spun around and raced after him. A steady beat pounded in her head. She heard someone scream- she didn't realize until Mike and Laura turned around, that it was her own enraged growl. She flung herself at Mike, claws drawn. Mike fell flat on his back. She scratched at his face and neck. People tried to pull her off, but she punched him square between the eyes.

Morgan felt an aching in her hand, then it became a burning with a loud crunch upon impact.

She felt strong hands grab her arms and rip her off the floor.

It was the principal.

As she was twirled around, Morgan saw Laura, staring in horror.

Morgan let her feet wail, and kicked Laura in the jaw, right under her chin. She sent her free falling across the hallway and hit the lockers.

Morgan was thrust into an office chair as angry adults stared at her.

Morgan's heart was pounding.

She felt cold and sweaty. Her eyelids felt like there were water droplets in the creases.

Morgan watched the school nurse pick up the phone on the desk and start dialing... mom.

Morgan felt so free. Everything spun in slow motion. She knew her chair was falling over. Mrs. Bradstreet tried to catch her. Morgan then closed her eyes and blacked out.

"And I'm losing all control now, and my hazard signs are all out. I'm asking you to show me what this life is all about. "

-Thousand foot Krutch

~ Chapter Fourteen ~

"This is a Call" Aaron Sprinkle \Joel Bruyere \Steve Augustine \Trevor McNevan © Flush on the Flop Music \Pockethood Publishing \Spinning Audio Vortex, Inc. \Teerawk Music Publishing \Thirsty Moon River Publishing Inc. \Whatthewhat Music Publishing

~ Chapter Fourteen ~

"Morgan, we need to go now!"

Morgan moaned as she alighted off her bed. Her pale face explained her feelings. Morgan had an appointment with the school counselor, principals, Mike, and his parents.

Laura wasn't going to be present because she didn't make a complaint, her face did it for her, but that was beside the point, Morgan could get suspended!

Morgan put her seatbelt on and gripped her stomach. In her gut she knew she was wrong, and she had lost control of herself, she would have to formally apologize. At the school steps, Morgan felt like she could cry, as she walked down the hallway she knew she wouldn't be able to open her mouth without breaking down, and that made her panic.

"Morgan, good news," Principal Richards began, "The Miganouski's will not be pressing charges…"

Morgan looked out of the corner of her eye at the Miganouski's sitting at the other end of the table.

"But they would like an explanation and a formal apology."

"Apology? Apology. Fine, they asked, they'll get it, but they'll be shocked when they hear my 'explanation'."

Everyone stared at Morgan expectantly.

Morgan recalled her morning…

A girl on the front steps looked at Morgan, and started whispering to her companion.

Then another, then another.

Morgan went through the metal detectors and realized there was a swarm of people looking at her, laughing.

Some said 'ho' or 'slut' other things she could hear were 'easy' and swear words. Morgan felt like she was going to fall over. Why were they saying this? Her head spun around her body. She felt like she was on a carousal horse. Her stomach was killing her, but she kept walking. She fidgeted self-consciously as she saw Mike walking down the hall.

Morgan had the feeling this would happen, but it didn't dull the shocking news she heard from the girls standing by her talking.

"They make such a great couple."

"Yeah, they've been going out for, like, a week!"

There he was, with Laura Sheen… he had cheated on her with Laura! Morgan's heart felt so much pain, then she felt nausea. It changed to rage as she grew closer to the couple. Then as she passed them, she felt defiance.

"I didn't do anything," she thought.

A creepy looking guy walked up to Morgan and whispered loud enough for a few around them to hear.

"So, I hear you paid Mike to have sex with you, what about me?"

Suddenly Morgan felt an emotion she never felt before-vengeance.

She wanted to hurt him the way he hurt her, she wanted pay back, he used her, then lied about her, while having a backup girl.

It wasn't fair, but she would make it that way.

Morgan spun around and raced after Mike. She would even the score, no matter what trouble it would get her into.

"That's not true!" Mike screamed, jumping out of his chair.

"Shut her up!"

Mike's parents stared at him in bewilderment. Morgan's mother was crying; the principal was listening intently while the vice principal was in shock and the counselor was writing something. Morgan continued.

"I'm sorry, Principal Richards, that I let my feelings get out of control. I apologize Mrs. Lawry, for causing such a ruckus in your school." Morgan addressed Mike's parents.

"I am sincerely sorry, Mr. Miganouski, that your son thinks so lowly of women, and that I let him use me. I'm sorry Mrs. Miganouski, that your son is a liar, a manipulator, a womanizer and… a sinner," Morgan added for affect. I apologize for realizing I could punish him, and that no one else would. I feel awful that I injured him, because he injured me, I deserved it ya know," Morgan sarcastically continued.

"I formally apologize, Mike, for kicking your new girlfriend instead of you!"

"Morgan, that's enough," her mother gently put her hand on Morgan's leg.

"Well, um, Morgan. Thank you for your honesty," Mrs. Lawry commented.

Mike's parents rose to leave, Morgan watched to see their reaction.

Shame, mourning, regret? Nope, uncertainty. How could they be uncertain that she was telling the truth?!

Morgan's mom led her to the doorway.

"Morgan will not need to be suspended, will she?" she asked Mr. Richards.

"Normally, yes, but after hearing that she was provoked in such a cynical and emotional way, we aren't. Plus, Mr. and Mrs. Miganouski aren't making a formal complaint."

"Thank you." Morgan's mom let the door shut as she led Morgan outside.

"Honey, how come you didn't tell me?"

"Because, I don't know. I can't talk to you about that kind of thing."

Morgan's mom started the car and turned in shock.

"What kind of thing?"

"Guys, boyfriends, sex."

"Why do you say that?" she asked, hurt.

Morgan was already defensive from the situation she just walked out of.

"All you do is complain about men, you put them down and say how awful they are. What image am I supposed to have? I have no perception of how real relationships are supposed to be anymore!"

"Morgan, don't talk like that! I've tried my best to raise you and prepare you for the real world."

"You certainly have made it 'real'!"

"Morgan, be quiet!"

"Why, I don't have the right to tell you what I need to survive?!"

"No Morgan, I am your mother, I know what you need."

"I don't even know why I am here," Morgan shrieked.

"Because you attacked your ex-boyfriend, Morgan," her mom returned coolly.

Morgan's rage was through the roof; she could stop a moving car right now.

"NO! I mean alive!"

Both women sat quietly for a while. Mrs. Parker stopped the car at a red light. She turned and addressed Morgan.

"What are you saying?" she asked quietly.

"I can't stand life anymore. I'm sick of this. I don't know why I'm even living."

Morgan's mom appeared to be in deep thought.

"Morgan, I think you need to see…"

Morgan interrupted her.

"No mom, I think you need to stop thinking you always know what I need, you don't!"

Morgan shifted in her seat, folded her arms, and looked out the window.

"I'm sorry, I don't understand."

"No kidding," Morgan stated.

Then Morgan could hear her mother crying.

"Mom, stop it, crying never fixed anything, you're always crying!"

Morgan regretted the words the second they came out of her mouth.

"Well, acting like a rock never got anyone anywhere either, Morgan."

Her mom shifted.

They got into the apartment and her mom went directly to her room.

Morgan rolled her eyes at herself.

"I'm so stupid, so immature," she thought.

"You're such a brat," a voice echoed in her mind. She agreed silently.

"You're so worthless; you'll never become anything more than that. Nothing. You're only made of the stuff people see."

Morgan recalled all the things people had said about her.

Unsure, bratty, ugly, undesirable, uncool, hard, and cold-hearted.

"I'm only worth what I appear to be to others," she thought.

"That would be nothing.

"If I'm to strong for some people, that's their problem."

-Glenda Jackson

~ Chapter Fifteen ~

~ Chapter Fifteen ~

Morgan wrapped her arms around her frigid body, staring at the moon. It seemed to look down and smile at her, which was unusual, because on most nights when the moon was full it looked like it was shocked.

Morgan breathed in the cold December air and exhaled watching the vapor from her breath dissipate among the tiny glistening snowflakes that were falling on the pavement. The frosty air burned her nose and cheeks, making them numb.

"Like me," she thought.

She repeated again and again to herself, "I'll never find anything I dream of."

Morgan wanted to cry so badly, but she couldn't make herself, like she didn't have the energy. She let out a tiny whimper and shifted in her spot.

"You'll never marry happily, you'll never find 'the one', you'll never have an ambition, you'll never go to school, and never be happy," she told herself.

"I'm ugly, stupid and selfish, who would want to deal with me? I'm worthless!" A tiny voice whispered in the air carried by the wind:

"Destiny lies in Him…"

Morgan whipped around. No one was there. The street lamp lit the sidewalk well enough to see about two streets down. No one was standing or walking away. She was all alone.

"I didn't say that," she thought, bewildered.

The wind blew sharply against her face. Morgan shut her eyes to protect them from the icy blast.

"Destiny lies in Him…"

"Who's there?" she squealed.

There was no answer.

"God?" she questioned.

"If you're really out there, say something."

She listened. Nothing happened.

"Figures God is never here when I need Him and He never answers when I want Him to."

Morgan turned around and went up the steps into her building. She climbed the stairs and went back into her apartment.

"Morgan, what were you doing outside?" her mother confronted her.

Morgan stood for a second.

"You weren't smoking, were you?!"

"Nooo…" Morgan answered.

"I was thinking."

"Good, because smoking is bad for you," her mother said pulling out her own pack.

"I know mom."

"It's a bad habit, don't be like me."

"I try not to," Morgan said.

She went into her room and sat down. Christmas was in three weeks. She had no money to buy any presents for anyone. She couldn't get a job. Most jobs around here were minimum wage and 16+ was the age requirement.

Morgan got changed and got ready for bed.

She tucked her feet under the covers and sat still before laying down.

"I wanted to be a figure skater," Morgan remembered, picking at a fuzzy on her pajama bottoms.

"I wanted to be famous, to be loved. Now I'm nobody."

She turned off her lamp and laid her head on the cold cotton pillow. Morgan breathed deeply to smell the fresh cold scent of fabric softener, and closed her eyes. Morgan listened all night to the whispers:

"Destiny lies in Him."

"My harp is turned to mourning,
and my flute to the voice of those
who weep."

-Job 30: 31

~ Chapter Sixteen ~

~ Chapter Sixteen ~

"Merry Christmas!" Mia said, handing Morgan a gift. Angela and Ryan were also at the school stairs.

"Here, this is all I could get," Morgan replied, thrusting the Christmas goody bags at them.

The bell rang announcing the beginning of sixth period.

Morgan rushed to her English class at full speed.

"Morgan, come here."

Morgan felt agony swelling inside her.

She turned around to face her English teacher, Miss. Carlet.

"Want to explain this?" she asked, placing a piece of paper on her desk.

Morgan recognized her handwriting on it, with a red pen scribbled all over it.

At the top was a big red D- with the comment, "very poor" added next to it. Morgan let out a huge huff and stepped closer, picking up the report.

"Morgan, I didn't give you an F because I know you can do better. After Christmas break, I expect an improvement."

"Sure," Morgan tried to reply enthusiastically, but she knew she couldn't.

It had been a long day, but it was finally over. Morgan threw her backpack on the kitchen chair and went to call Angela.

"Morgan!"

"Oh no!" Morgan thought.

Morgan placed the phone back into its cradle.

"Huh?" she asked as her mother stormed in.

"I got a call from your Spanish teacher last night…"

Morgan thought about where this was going.

"He says you are going to flunk out."

Flunk out. Those were terrifying words.

"How?" Morgan spat out.

"You tell me," her mother returned, slamming the utensils drawer.

"I've been working hard," Morgan whined.

She didn't mean for it to come out that way. It was more of a desperate cry to escape.

"What are we going to do?" her mother prodded.

Morgan stood with her head hung.

"Morgan, answer me."

"If I say anything, you'll get mad at me."

"Why would I get mad, I asked you a question for God's sake, answer it!"

"You'll just tell me I'm stupid and I don't care, or I'm not trying so I'll say it first, ok? There!"

Morgan stormed out of the room and slammed the door. She wasn't going to help make Christmas dinner.

"Mom can do it all by herself for all I care. She just belittles me when I do, anyway."

Morgan stayed in her room all Saturday and Saturday night. She came out to watch TV on Sunday morning with Adam. Morgan's mom was in the kitchen when the phone rang.

"Thursday? That's fine," Morgan heard.

"Ok mom, bye bye." She hung up the phone.

Morgan dared not ask who it was.

"Adam, go ask mommy if Grandma and Grandpa are coming over," Morgan coaxed, pushing Adam off the couch. Morgan flipped the station to VH1. Nothing good was on so she surfed through the channels twice and turned the television off. She peered into the kitchen and saw Adam wasn't in there. He never asked.

"Was that Grandma?" Morgan asked, licking batter from the counter off her finger.

"Uhuh."

"Are they coming down?"

"For Christmas they are," her mom replied with an annoyed tone.

Morgan promptly left the room.

It was Christmas Eve. Morgan's grandparents were comfortably set up on the living room couch. Morgan's mom was arranging the Christmas tree ornaments. The family neatly put all the beads and dangly things on the tree, and Grandpa put the gold star on top. The group continued with a feast and a movie after.

As the end credits rolled, Morgan got up and lifted the sleepy

Adam off the couch. She carried him into his room and placed him on his bed. She took his shoes and shirt off and put a nightshirt on.

While she buttoned it, Morgan noticed a flashing light on the wall, reflecting from outside. It looked like a piece of glass was being reflected off a street lamp.

Morgan slowly crept to the window.

She could hear someone outside singing.

It was a lullaby. It's minor melody floated around the room eerily and back down the street. Morgan recognized it as the one she heard her mother humming sometimes.

Morgan was confused.

The light was gone, the humming was gone, but there was nothing there in the first place. Morgan went down the hall and said good night to her grandparents. Her grandmother seemed extremely pale and tired. Morgan figured she was fatigued by the trip. She went back to her room and climbed into her bed and turned off the light.

Flashes of a dark room flooded her mind.

Two glowing eyes stared at her.

A face walked through the darkness.

The figure was in the form of a black wolf. It had green eyes and its teeth protruded from its mouth like fangs.

"I told you," it said slyly.

Then it laughed and snarled, with its nose turned up. Then suddenly, it snapped its head down, looking at her and lunged forward to attack.

Morgan screamed.

There on top of her sat a pudgy little four-year-old boy, staring in wonder.

"It's Christmas, come on!" Adam yelled. He jumped off and ran out of the room. Morgan's face was wet with sweat and her palms were sticky.

"I told you," echoed in her mind.

"Told me what?" she wondered.

What did her dream represent?

Morgan sauntered into the living room and sat down on the floor next to the Christmas tree. Her mom put on a Christmas c.d. in the stereo and everyone sat down and opened presents. Morgan was happy to see her grandparents. She hadn't seen them since her birthday this past summer. Morgan's mother alighted and handed her a present. Morgan ripped the delicate tissue paper and opened the box. Inside laid a crisp new dress. Then she got another and a pair of jeans, a sweater, and Evanescence's new album. Morgan's grandparents gave her a shirt with an embroidered butterfly on the front and bell sleeves.

Morgan observed her brother screaming when he opened a set of Lego's. He was so happy, carefree, believed everyone was good and right; that everything existed to make him happy and every person around him had good intentions.

Then Morgan's mother slowly stepped forward and handed Morgan a jewelry case.

"Morgan, uh, this, um…" she stuttered.

"This is from your father, and, um, he sent it with this card."

She gently put the card in Morgan's hand and returned to her seat, pretending to examine the wrapping paper on the gift next to her.

The card revealed little more than the printed message.

"May this season bring you many joys, Merry Christmas, Dad," she read dryly.

Then she opened the box.

It revealed a charm for a bracelet.

"What is it dear?" her grandmother prodded.

"It's a heart locket charm."

It would be nice if he even cared to ask you if you had a bracelet for the charm," her mother snapped.

"Honey," grandma started.

"Mitch tries, you must accept the fact that he wants a new life, and he knows he still has obligations to the kids, but when he left you, he left them. You know as well as I do, he doesn't want to talk to you anyway."

"I know mom."

"God is using him as a test of your strength, He is working to bless you in the end."

"Anyone want coffee?" Morgan's mother interrupted, and stepped into the kitchen.

Morgan was intrigued by what her grandmother said. Could that be the answer to her prayer? Could it be that God used circumstances and problems to prove He was there? Could it be that He was watching and waiting?

"Honey, we have another gift for you."

"Uh, oh, thank you."

Morgan tried to focus back on the moment.

The gift proved to be a silver chain necklace and an envelope with $50 in it.

"So you can buy whatever else you would like," Grandpa said.

"Or buy something for your girlfriends," Grandma added.

"Or your boyfriend?" Grandpa winked.

"Dad, she doesn't have a boyfriend," Morgan's mom called from in the kitchen.

Morgan decided to call Mia, she had a big family, so it didn't matter if the phone rang too.

"Hello?"

"Is Mia there?"

"Sure, hold on," Mia's sister said, slamming the phone down. Morgan pulled the phone away from her ear to lessen the impact.

"Morgan?"

"Yep," Morgan answered.

"What's up?"

"I had a dream last night," Morgan explained.

"Ooo, tell me!"

"Well, there was a wolf standing in a dark room, it was big, black, and its teeth came out over its lips, and its eyes were green."

Mia listened in suspense.

"It looked at me and said, 'I told you', then it started laughing at me."

"That's it?" Mia questioned.

"It lunged at me after, then Adam came in and woke me up, so I couldn't finish it.

Mia thought, then concluded,

"I think I know what it means."

Morgan expected a joking explanation, but listened.

"The wolf is a spirit, an evil spirit, that is trying to convince you of something, and is telling you that he succeeded. You're in a spiritual battle, Morgan. Something wants you really bad, because someone else does."

Morgan stood at the kitchen table, stunned.

"What do I do?" she asked stupidly.

"I know you hate the idea, but won't you come to church with me sometime?"

Morgan hesitantly agreed then hung up.

Morgan walked into the living room.

"Where's Grandma and Grandpa?" Morgan asked, observing her mother's crestfallen face.

"They left," her mother sniffled.

Morgan became alarmed.

"What's wrong?"

Silence filled the air for a long time.

"Mom? Is everything ok?"

"No honey, something bad has happened."

Morgan's mind raced. She took a seat on the piano bench.

"Your grandmother is very sick. She just told me… that she had been diagnosed with a rapid growing bone cancer.

"Oh, that's bad," Morgan replied, trying to come up with an answer.

"Morgan, they can't treat it, the doctors are telling her she's…"

Morgan picked at the black plastic bench she sat on while her mother heaved a heavy sigh.

"She's going to die."

Morgan was filled with such grief, but to show her pain would only make the whole family's stability just crumble. She had to prove she was strong. Staring at the floor, she listened to her mother's sobs. A tear fell from her own face.

"God, how could you do this?" she questioned.

Morgan sat stiff in her seat. Rage filled her whole body. It filled her stomach and her throat; it invaded her head until she felt like she could explode.

She rose and ran out of the room, slamming the world out.

Everything around her was crumbling.

"I told you," echoed in her head.

"Shut up!" She screamed.

"I don't care, I don't care."

"I hate you." she clenched her fists, rocking on the floor.

If she could only erase everything that happened this year.

If only she could die instead.

"You can't be brave if you've only had good things happen to you."

-Mary Tyler Moore

~ Chapter Seventeen ~

~ Chapter Seventeen ~

"Hey Morgan," Angela said, stepping next to her at her locker.

Morgan swung her locker door shut.

"What's wrong?" Angela asked.

"Everything! My life is ruined! My dad is gone, my grades are bad, my grandmother is dying, and I have no…"

"Wait, wait, hold on Morgan," Angela interrupted.

"Your grandmother? Why? How?"

"She has cancer."

"Ohmigod."

"Yeah," Morgan heaved.

"Morgan I am so sorry."

"So am I," Morgan said, then she took her bag and walked down the hall.

Some girls were in the hall corners, gossiping.

One stepped forward, walking beside Morgan, while the others trailed.

"So how was it?" she asked.

"What?" Morgan asked clueless.

"Mike Miganouski," she continued.

Morgan cringed.

"It's a rumor, ok? I never did it with him, I never have! I am a virgin, ok?!" she yelled.

The girls stopped. Morgan looked around; people were staring at her now. Morgan's face turned fire red as she ran away and galloped down the sidewalk. Her mind was like a radio trying to find a station. All she got was fuzz.

Where was her life going?

She stood in the courtyard by the bus pickup, thinking.

"Who am I really?"

"Morgan?!"

Ryan ran up to her.

"Hey, what's up? I heard, um, I heard," he stammered.

"Ryan, please, I don't want to talk."

"It would be better if…"

"Ryan, I said go away!" she shouted.

Ryan stood, shocked, then turned and walked over the snow bank onto the sidewalk.

Tears poured down Morgan's pale face. She let her hands hang limp, and she stared at the swirling clouds above.

Then she heard a whistle.

"Yoww! There goes the virgin."

"Oh, God please," she begged.

"Hey baby," one said walking past her.

Another, on the other side of her ran his finger along her cheek.

"Look, she's crying, poor girly."

Morgan huffed and slung her bag over her shoulder with all her might letting it hit him, knocking him over. Now he was the object of ridicule as she escaped.

"Just keep walking, don't look," she told herself.

She slowly walked home. Why should she hurry?

A voice from deep within her being started speaking.

"I told you, you aren't beautiful, no one wants you, and you're selfish, stupid, undesirable, you're worth nothing to them. I told you so.

Morgan started running.

The adrenaline pumped through her veins as she raced down the street.

She was running from the voice.

It chased after her as she ran.

"Go away! Stop it!" she screamed.

She turned around to see, it was still chasing her.

Morgan got onto her street and ran up her front steps, went in, and closed the door. She turned around, looking outside, nothing was there.

"You're going insane," she told herself.

Morgan, exhausted, walked up the stairs into her apartment.

She sat down on her bed and soaked in the quiet. She liked it this way. "Where there is nothing, I can be nothing."

Then she heard her mother walk in, someone was with her. Morgan opened her eyes to listen. She couldn't hear if she couldn't see. It was a guy, he was laughing and talking. Morgan dared not come out of her room. Her mom probably thought she wasn't home yet.

"Why is it she always has to have a guy now?" Morgan questioned.

She crept over to her door and kneeled, slowly turning the doorknob and opening the door. She listened to their conversation for a while, gaining nothing important except that the guy's name was Kevin and that he had to work tomorrow.

Whatever.

Morgan got up and returned to her homework.

She couldn't concentrate at all.

Then she heard the door shut.

"Morgan?" her mother shouted.

Morgan didn't know what to expect.

"The greater part of our happiness or misery depends on our dispositions, and not on our circumstances."

- Martha Washington

~ Chapter Eighteen ~

Last words "Happiness"
Woman's Day magazine Produced by Anne Louise Fritz
September 1st 2004 67th year 14th issue page 162

~ Chapter Eighteen ~

Morgan walked into the kitchen cautiously.

"Oh, you are home," Morgan's mom commented.

"Who was that?"

"Who was who?" her mom asked obliviously.

"The guy. Kevin."

"Oh, um, well, I think he likes me!" her mom answered enthusiastically.

Morgan just watched her mom's face evolve back as she addressed Morgan.

"I need you to watch Adam tonight, and please, no phone."

"Ok."

"We are going out for dinner, I'm going to leave soon, so I'm going to have to take a shower and dress."

"Going out, again," Morgan thought, after her mom left the room.

"Why does she have to do this? Always making plans without asking me if I have something planned, I never do, but it's the principle!"

Morgan's mom reappeared in a black pantsuit on with her hair back in a tight bun.

Morgan was sitting, watching TV.

"Be back by 9:00, bye."

"Hm," Morgan answered and waved over her back.

As her mom left, Morgan picked up the phone and called Mia.

It was the answering machine.

"I just wanted to tell you I'll be at your house Sunday for… church… just call me back and tell me when to get there, ok, bye."

Morgan hung up and gave Adam dinner.

Mia called back.

"Hey."

"Hm."

"I'd say come here about 9:30, ok?"

"Yeah."

"Ok… bye."

"Hm."

Morgan hung up. She knew she was rude, but she had no energy to be happy. Everything in her life seemed so gray and monotone. Maybe this was the pick-me-up she needed.

Morgan cleaned the kitchen and put Adam to bed. She didn't want to sleep; she knew it would be torture for her. Voices and creatures would chase her in her dreams. She sat down on the couch and watched CNN.

She felt tired and stretched her arms with a great big yawn.

Morgan laid her head down on a soft pillow and stared at the white walls until they looked fuzzy and faded away.

Morgan sat up, she heard breathing behind her. Slowly she turned and saw a small figure crouched in the corner; it wasn't Adam.

It was a girl. The girl was extremely thin and pale.

Most of her was naked and dirty.

Morgan rubbed her eyes and kneeled over the back of the couch, leaning on the armrest. The girl was looking down at her knees, breathing heavily. Her breaths were labored and gurgling. The girl then looked up slowly and stared at Morgan.

Then Morgan was alarmed. The girls' hair was short, brown, and very messy. Her face- her face... Morgan could pass out.

Her face was Morgan's face, and the girl knew it. She stared at Morgan, then opened her mouth, slowly saying, "Come back to me. Don't leave me. You have lost me, and replaced me for the world."

"Who are you?" Morgan replied.

The girls' green eyes sparkled in the darkness. She leaned forward in a whisper, "You're heart."

Morgan sat up; she immediately looked over into the corner. Nothing was there.

"Humph, this is what I get for falling asleep!"

Morgan noticed the TV was off and her mom's door was shut. So she had come home. Morgan got off the couch and went into the kitchen to find it was after midnight.

Morgan unlocked the door and went out. She got up onto the roof and stared up at the stars. If only she could be one of them. Morgan sat down on the cold cement. She started to hum the tune in her head. She sang it out loud, she sang it hard, for as long as she could. It was like a cry for help from the deepest part of her soul. She let it reach the highest heaven and reverberate back into her throat. What was this lullaby that followed her? What was the meaning of her dream?

"Is that the condition of my heart?"

Morgan's head spun and she felt chills run down her spine. She felt as if she was being watched. Morgan got up and looked around before going back in. Morgan lay down, outstretched on her bed. A cold tear ran down her temple.

She couldn't go on for much longer.

"….Fragments of my life are shattered here, the vines choke me out."

- Ashley Lauren Boettcher

~ Chapter Nineteen ~

~ Chapter Nineteen ~

L ast night was a night Morgan didn't want to relive. In fact, this whole week wasn't too great. No, her whole life had been a misery. Morgan was happy the weekend was finally here. Ryan and Mia walked to the bus together without saying goodbye to her.

"It's your own fault," she told herself.

Morgan caught sight of Angela through the mob.

"Angela," she called.

Angela turned around expectantly.

"Why did Ryan and Mia leave so suddenly?" Morgan asked once she caught up.

"Because you told them to leave you alone. Man, you have problems Morgan."

Morgan stopped walking, letting Angela continue. People bumped and shoved against Morgan. Was she that cold? Now she couldn't stand herself anymore. She really needed to find herself. Her life was amounting to nothing and she was lost in a world that didn't need anymore "Morgans".

Sunday morning, Morgan put on her new jeans and a blouse and walked to Mia's house, which was located in the wealthy section of Brooklyn.

Morgan knocked three times on the door.

Mia answered.

"You ready?" Mia asked.

"Yeah, sure- I am here."

"Ok, ok smarty."

They walked four blocks to the small church; it was a far cry from Brooklyn Tabernacle. It housed little more than 100 people. Mia found Morgan and herself a seat in the middle on the far right side of the church.

Morgan felt prickly sensations all over her body as she read the banner that was hung over the pulpit.

"Destiny lies in Him."

"In God," she said out loud.

"Hm?" Mia asked.

"Nothing- I, er, I'm praying."

"Ah, so was I," Mia replied.

Quiet meditative piano chords were being played in the background.

The assistant pastor then came forward and greeted everyone.

There was singing of a few songs, which Morgan mouthed the words to, and then the sermon.

Morgan put on an attentive face and spaced out.

Then Morgan realized people were rising to leave, Morgan sat up, trying to look aware.

"So what did you think?" Mia asked.

"Honestly?"

Mia nodded.

"Lame-o."

"Well, youth group is on Friday night...?"

"Ok, we can try that."

"This week?" Mia questioned enthusiastically.

"Hmm, ok," Morgan agreed.

Mia and Morgan walked home. Morgan dropped Mia off then continued to her own house.

Morgan raced up the stairs and unlocked her apartment. She could hear her mom yelling at someone.

"Don't ever do that! Ever again!"

"Hello?" Morgan called sheepishly.

Morgan's mother appeared around the corner.

"Morgan Ann, I need you to be watching him! Where were you all morning?"

"At church."

"At church?" her mother questioned doubtfully.

"Why?"

"Mia invited me."

"Oh."

"Morgan, say hello to Kevin."

Morgan stepped over Adam whimpering on the floor, recovering from some fit.

"Hi," he said.

Morgan observed. Kevin had dark eyes and hair, very tan skin and a massive build. He looked like a fireman or athlete who went to the gym a little too much.

"Uh uh," she acknowledged him.

He thrust his hand out for a shake, but Morgan just stared at it.

She liked to intimidate intimidating men. He pulled his hand back and cleared his throat.

Morgan's mom led her to the couch.

The three sat down.

"So um, Kevin is a boxing teacher!" her mother tried to push the conversation.

"I really need to go homework, mom."

"Morgan!"

"I don't have time, sorry."

Morgan got up and firmly walked out.

Really, she had no homework; she just didn't want to be around Kevin.

He seemed very unlikable, but Morgan couldn't put her finger on it.

Something about his disposition bothered her, but she would soon find out.

"When life hands you a lemon say,
' Oh yeah, I like lemons, what else
ya got?' "

-Henry Rollins

~ Chapter Twenty ~

*Taken from "The Sisterhood of the Traveling Pants" by Ann Brashares.
Delacorte Press- an imprint of Random House Children's Books, a division of
Random House, Inc.*

Used with permission.

~ Chapter Twenty ~

L ater that week on Friday morning, Morgan awoke and found her mom in the kitchen eating. The doorbell rang and Morgan jumped up, expecting one of her friends, but it wasn't- it was Kevin.

Morgan purposely rolled her eyes and moved out of the doorway. "Hey everyone."

Kevin handed Mrs. Parker a bouquet of roses. She didn't look at him.

"Apparently they had a fight last night," Morgan thought.

"Come on Sarah, I'm sorry. I said I was sorry."

Morgan's mom continued munching on her Chex. Adam was eating (more like dropping) Cheerios.

"Sarah!" Kevin hollered.

"Kevin, I don't feel like..."

Kevin screamed out a swear and pounded his fist on the table.

Morgan observed how his fingers notched into a ball; how they all interlocked into a tight fist; how nothing could stop it- nothing ever. She was filled with fear.

"Kids, leave," Morgan's mom directed.

Morgan led Adam out of the room, stopping short, herself.

Kevin got in her face and screamed, "GO!"

She could smell whiskey on his breath. She could almost barf. For some reason she didn't; she turned and fled.

Screaming adults were left in the kitchen.

This brought back severe memories.

"It wouldn't be so bad if he left," she thought.

Morgan couldn't make out any of the words, so she walked over to the doorway.

Then she heard a huge SMACK and her mother cry out in pain.

Morgan's brain went into spasms.

"Now that just isn't allowed," she said.

Morgan's mind obeyed her body as her eyes scanned for a weapon. She picked up her tennis racket and plowed down the hallway. She was afraid of her own pounding feet.

Morgan kicked Adam's Lego stuff out of her way and rammed her way through the mess into the kitchen.

She found her mom cowering on the floor, with the chair toppled over next to her. Kevin was leaning over, ready for an umpteenth blow.

Morgan's rage bursted through.

"No you don't!" she screeched.

She scrambled to her mom's side and imagined Kevin's head was a tennis ball. She smacked him hard, sending him against the counter.

He growled and ran after her.

Morgan lifted the racket in the form of a backhand into his nose.

She spun the racket around and hit the side of his head with the frame.

He leaned back and she kicked him in the groin.

He screamed and smashed Morgan into the wall as he bent in pain. He kicked her mom in the stomach and turned for the door.

Morgan raced after him and he turned and, there, headed for her was that great big, tight interlocking fist, she felt fear, then nothing.

Morgan found herself sprawled across the floor, arms out like she had been crucified. The back of her head pounded from the impact of her fall. The front of her face ached from his impact. Her mom was cradling ice in her hand, trying to get more, but her hands were shaking so hard she managed to drop everything she touched. She burst into tears, continuing to wipe out everything in the freezer.

Morgan got up and assisted her.

"How long has this been going on?" Morgan screamed.

Her mother sobbed.

"Oh God!" Morgan called out.

"I don't know. He only does this when he drinks."

"How often would that be?" Morgan interrogated.

The yelling made Morgan's head feel lofty, so she sat down. Across from her was the oven door. She could see her reflection. She had a big purple swipe under her eye.

Morgan wasn't scared anymore. She was determined to stop him from hurting her family. This was revenge for all the men in her life hurting her.

She figured since her mom was just getting ice when she came to, she wasn't out for long.

Morgan got up and ran out, down the steps and out onto sidewalk.

She was in a hot pursuit.
Step one- find him.
Step two- find a cop.
Both were accomplished in one breath.
"Thank you God."

"Life is either a daring adventure
or nothing. "

-Helen Keller

~ Chapter Twenty-One ~

~ Chapter Twenty-One ~

Morgan raced down the street screaming, "Police! Police! Help!"

She caught the attention of a bicycle policeman.

"Get him!" she cried out, pointing.

Kevin turned around and looked at Morgan.

Was he laughing?

"He is!" Morgan thought.

She stopped running and froze in her place, terrified.

The police officer rode to Kevin and the girl.

"What's going on here?" he questioned.

"Nothing Joe, she's just confused."

"You know him?!" she questioned.

"Sure, I train in his class," the policeman answered.

"Why were you so upset?"

Kevin answered for her.

"Morgan's mother and I were fighting, and she was picking up the breakfast dishes and slipped. Morgan was mistaken, thinking I would ever hurt her mother, isn't that right Morgan?"

Kevin stared straight into Morgan's eyes, then gestured with his eyes to his hidden fist.

"Y... yes, right."

"Ok, how did you get the black eye then?" the man questioned gravely.

"Um," Morgan looked at Kevin, then at her feet.

"A girl at school yesterday."

"Ok then folks, everything is fine here, right?"

"Right," Kevin answered.

"See you Monday!" Then the officer peddled away.

Kevin turned to leave in his car.

"You can't lie forever," Morgan challenged.

Kevin looked up and laughed.

He got in his car and drove away, making puddles splash at Morgan's feet.

Morgan looked down to check the time- she was late for school.

"Why even bother now?"

Morgan walked back home and found her mom watching TV on

the couch.

"Don't you have work?" Morgan asked.

"I called in sick," her mother replied, shoving popcorn in her mouth.

"Don't talk about this, stay out of it, I'll deal with it on my own."

"Mom, I'm already involved, he hit me too, remember? If I let you handle this, you'll end up dead in an alley."

"Morgan!"

"I'm serious!" Morgan continued.

"You need to get help before you have to go into witness protection or something!"

"Morgan, you're going to be late for school!"

"I already am," she replied.

"You need to go, please!" Morgan's mother begged.

"Fine, but you must lock the door."

"Morgan, he isn't dangerous!"

"He isn't?" Morgan questioned in disbelief.

"He just sent you flying and knocked me on my back, with the intention of continuing, and he's not dangerous?!"

"He only does this when he's drunk, like when he's upset, or we fight," Morgan's mother whimpered.

"So that's 90% of the time. Great, good choice mom."

Morgan slammed the door and ran off to school. She didn't bother trying to cover her black eye with make-up, she thought maybe the counselor would see and ask, but no one noticed.

Morgan was invisible, as always.

When Morgan got home, her mother was panicked, getting her purse and keys.

"Morgan, hurry up, get Adam!"

"Why? What's going on?" Morgan asked, spinning around, trying to watch her mother run in all directions.

"Your grandfather called, grandma is in the hospital."

"Oh no!" Morgan cried out.

She ran and got Adam and a book for him to look at.

The two ran down the steps, Morgan carrying Adam.

Kevin was on his way up. Morgan's mom stopped and looked at Kevin regretfully.

"What's the hurry?" he asked innocently.

"My mother is in the hospital."

"Come on, I'll drive," Kevin offered.

Mrs. Parker turned and looked at Morgan and shrugged.

They packed into Kevin's Eclipse and drove to the hospital in 20 minutes.

Morgan's mom raced to the nurses' station at the Emergency Room.

"I'm trying to find my mother, Beatrice Thompson; she came in her with her husband."

The nurse calmly addressed the group.

"You need to go upstairs, she should have been admitted- she is the woman with the cancer, right?"

"Yes."

"Ok, second floor, just tell them the same thing."

Morgan's mom stomped over to the elevator just as it shut.

She growled in frustration and pressed the 'up' button.

Once they got there, she calmed down.

Kevin led the way to grandma's room.

She was in her room, quietly sleeping with an IV. She had two bags of fluid being pumped into her.

Morgan felt nauseated at the smell of 'hospital'.

She looked over at her grandfather, seated beside her grandmother, holding her hand.

He looked up, tears streaming down his face.

Morgan almost fell over. He never cried.

"The real things haven't changed. It is still best to be honest and truthful; to make the best of what we have; to be happy with simple pleasures, and to have courage when things go wrong."

-Laura Ingalls Wilder

~ Chapter Twenty-Two ~

"Sweet Thoughts"
Woman's Day Magazine May 14th 2002 65th year
9th issue page 111

~ Chapter Twenty-Two ~

Morgan's mother dropped her bag and rushed to her father's side.

"Dad, is everything ok?"

"Oh honey…" he said stroking her face.

Morgan watched a nurse walk in with another IV bag. It was red and it had the letter A negative on it.

"She's become anemic?" Morgan asked.

"Not just that, it's hard to explain honey, but she needs her sleep, so let's step out," her grandfather suggested.

They all stood in the hall, devastated.

"Are the doctors expecting her to recover from this?" Kevin asked coldly.

"Yes, but if she isn't tested and watched carefully she may not…"

Morgan's grandfather broke down and hid his face; Adam started wailing, just because his grandpa was.

Morgan sucked up the aching feeling in her stomach that would evolve into tears.

Then the doctor arrived.

"The results from the MRI are back, it looks like she may be a good candidate for radiation."

"Radiation is needed?" Morgan's mother asked.

"Well, only if your family and the patient consents. It will slow the progression of the disease by 60%."

Everyone stood quietly. They knew 'slow the progression' didn't mean cure.

"Multiple myeloma is a deadly cancer, but if treated correctly, your wife will live comfortably for several more years," the doctor said, addressing grandpa.

"I will have to talk to her."

"What will happen if she doesn't use any treatments?" Mrs. Parker asked.

"She will die," the doctor said gravely.

"I know, I know, but what is the progression like, how will… it happen?"

The doctor shifted uncomfortably.

"What she is experiencing now is bone pain, anemia, weakening, and abnormal cell production."

He paused, then continued.

"Further risks may be organ failure, if the infected cells spread. It usually invades the kidneys or spleen."

Morgan rolled her eyes in utter disbelief. Morgan's mom turned around and covered her eyes with her hand.

"Multiple myeloma interferes with blood flow to the skin, nose, toes, and fingers because it thickens the blood, so left untreated, she may have brain damage as well."

Morgan's grandfather looked up from the floor and started speaking.

"I don't think she will want any sort of therapy involving radiation."

"Then sir, our job is to make her comfortable until her time comes."

Morgan jerked her head down to avoid eye contact with anyone.

"The nurses have business cards available for you, if you need the number of any family counselors, they are at the nurses' station."

Morgan's mom groaned and buried her head in Kevin's chest.

"I'll be around if you have any more questions."

"Thank you," Morgan's grandfather said, stepping out of his leaned position against the wall.

"I know she won't take chemotherapy or radiation, she'll refuse."

"We will have to make her, dad. Please stop saying that!" Morgan's mom whined.

"The doctors said this is just a small problem, she should be out soon."

"I hope so," Morgan's mom said.

"So do I," Morgan thought, but she doubted anything good would happen after this, knowing her life's pattern.

"In youth we learn, in age we understand. "

- Marie von Ebner - Eschenbach

~ Chapter Twenty-Three ~

~ Chapter Twenty-Three ~

The banality of Morgan's life was taking its toll. She walked down school halls limp and hollow. She never spoke, she never felt, she never loved.

Morgan was confused as to why she even went to school.

She couldn't even remember when she enjoyed it.

Angela stood next to Morgan, perplexed, scrutinizing her every move.

"How's your grandma?" Angela asked.

Morgan turned.

"She's home now."

"I'll send a card," Angela commented.

"Hey!"

Ryan sauntered up to the two girls lockers.

"Angela, Mia and I are going to youth group tomorrow night-wanna come?"

"Sure, Morgan?"

"Huh?" Morgan looked up from her social science book.

"You want to come to church tomorrow night?"

"Ok, since I couldn't make it last week."

"Exactly," Ryan said enthusiastically, and left.

"I'll see you in class."

Morgan nodded and watched Angela walk away. She noticed Angela's hair had an added color this week. The vibrant purple emphasized the lipstick slathered on her mouth.

Morgan picked up her geometry book and slowly walked to class. The bell rang; Morgan walked in the door after.

"You're late, Parker," Mr. Anderson commented, and marked her down.

"Ok people..."

Mr. Anderson addressed the class with a piece of chalk in his hand.

"In a given dilatation, O is the center, A is mapped onto A-, um, B is mapped onto B-, and C is mapped onto C-, so... find the indicated measure if the scale factor is ¼."

Morgan watched him scribble the numbers and letters on the

board while her head spun.

"What is a dilatation?" she thought.

Morgan rubbed her forehead and bounced her pencil on the paper in front of her and closed her eyes.

"Dilatation…"

Morgan raised her hand.

"What is a dilatation?"

She could hear people laughing at her.

"A transformation that maps the points in a plane to the image points in relation to a fixed point. Let's say p is…"

Morgan tuned him out.

"Fixed points, image points, mapped points? What is that supposed to do for me? That's not a proper definition!"

Morgan threw her head back and stretched.

She looked around, repulsed to see Mike Miganouski and Michelle Reuben in the back, flirting together.

Then the bell rang. Morgan walked out to her locker with Mia at her side.

"Unbelievable," Morgan muttered.

"What?" Mia questioned.

"Mike and Michelle are dating now?"

"Yeah, I know."

"I just don't get it, I get everything dumped on me! It's like I'm cursed!"

The two stopped at Mia's locker.

"What do you mean?" she quizzed.

"First, my parents divorced, we move, I get stuck with my little brother to take care of, and my mom is going through the worst men she can find. Now with my grandma dying, I'm totally lost! Why? Why me?!"

Mia put her books in her locker space.

"People make mistakes, we make choices, that's the way God made us."

"And He chooses for my grandmother to die a horrible and painful death and torture me my whole life?"

"No!" Mia corrected.

"He does these things, allows trials and hardships to refine you, to mold you. He said that we are His clay, and He is the potter. If you try to take control, what you become will never work. Life is about living for God, not ourselves."

Morgan put her geometry book down to listen.

"You must accept your circumstances and work around them, for a better attitude, and for a better life."

"So He's trying to teach me a lesson?" Morgan asked.

"You have the wrong perspective," Mia stated, frustrated.

"God chooses to take your grandmother in His time, and He chooses to take her by cancer, to teach you to trust or listen to Him; so He can reveal to you your purpose in this life. Stay open Morgan, He's waiting for you to hear."

Then the bell rang, and Morgan understood.

Friday night opened with prayer and then a lot of singing, Morgan liked the songs; they were a lot less stingy than Sunday morning service's songs. Morgan listened to the sermon; it was about the Ten Commandments.

"Now you may think God is about a lot of rules and 'thou shalt nots', but that's the beauty of it all, He made these 'rules' because He wanted us to stay away from mistakes…"

"I've already made too many mistakes," Morgan thought to herself as the youth pastor continued.

"He's calling you…"

"Oh yeah? I don't hear Him," Morgan replied in her head.

"Reach out to Him tonight."

"How do I do that?" Morgan proceeded to talk in her head.

"Let's pray."

Morgan lowered her head, but looked around, watching everyone else, some were crying, other people her age were on their knees.

"I would never do that! Make such a scene!" Morgan thought.

"If you prayed that prayer tonight, just raise your hand so I know, thank you, yes, I see you… thank you… yes, any others?"

"What prayer? Who prayed what prayer?" Morgan thought, bewildered. Morgan's motherly side popped into her head.

"If you weren't talking, you would know!"

"Whatever," she retorted.

Morgan saw some more people raise their hands; she felt guilty looking, when she wasn't supposed to. It was an unwritten rule not to look at people during prayer.

After the prayer closed and the service ended, Morgan stayed silent.

She thought she understood yesterday, but now she had forgotten what it was she understood.

Could it possibly be, that she understood God? Or was it that He understood her?

Morgan went home still thinking. Her mother and Kevin were standing in the kitchen; as Morgan opened the door, her mother took a blow.

"Shut that door!" Kevin hollered.

"Where were you?" he confronted her.

"Church."

"Oh church, that's real interesting…" Kevin mocked.

"Get out of here!"

Morgan stood dazed.

"Go on! Get!"

He stepped forward, threatening to hit her face, and Morgan ran into her room. No,

Morgan was mistaken, how could she possibly understand God, or even more unbelievably, how could she even think He understood her. Or her life.

"Time- Our youth- It never really goes, does it? It is all held in our minds. "

-Helen Hooven Santmyre

~ Chapter Twenty-Four ~

~ Chapter Twenty-Four ~

Morgan watched the news as a fat man in a Victorian looking suit held up a frightened ground hog, declaring spring was here. Morgan looked outside.

"Doesn't look like it to me." She commented.

The snowy streets below were busy with whatever they did on a cold February afternoon. Morgan was waiting for her mom to come home. As always, she was late. Since she started going out with Kevin she made it a habit of eating at some fancy restaurant and not telling Morgan. She really wished he'd just go away. Vivid pictures of Kevin hitting her, her mom and Adam popped into her mind.

"I hate you." She said, hoping the message would reach him.

Suddenly, Morgan's mom and Kevin walked through the door.

"Hey Honey." Morgan's mom greeted. They had bags in their arms.

"Move!" Kevin commanded, gesturing that he wanted to put the bags where Morgan sat. Morgan escaped to her room and waited until Kevin left, to come out. She found her mom at the freezer, putting ice-cream away.

"Morgan," Her mother addressed her, wiping her frosty hands on her pants.

"You were very rude."

"To.....?" Morgan asked.

"To Kevin."

Morgan thought about what to say, a lot of words popped into her head, but she immediately swallowed them. Her mother continued accosting her.

"You need to straighten out, I can't believe you've been acting like this! Trying to get him arrested, hitting him with a tennis....."

Morgan interrupted her mother.

"Like how he hit you? How he threw a chair at you? How he kicked Adam to the floor the other day, and how he knocked me out? I don't have the right to be rude?"

"You don't understand this relationship Morgan!" Her mom yelled, slamming the egg carton on the counter.

"You are so jaded you don't even realize what you're doing to this family!"

Morgan's mom rushed over and grabbed Morgan's shoulders, pinning her to the wall.

"Life isn't fun and games, Morgan! Life isn't perfect. Stop living in a fairytale- this is the way men act! Deal with it!"

She loosed her grip letting Morgan jolt back when she pushed off her shoulders.

You need to stop being so naïve."

"Oh, right…." Morgan mocked.

"Young lady, one more word and you'll get….."

"Get what mom?!" Morgan screamed.

"Get grounded? I don't have a life! Get arrested, do drugs, get thrown out? It's better than being here. One more word and ……. What? You'll kill me?"

Morgan's mom put down a box of Hamburger Helper and turned around.

"Stop screaming." She said quietly.

"Stop screaming!?" Morgan wailed.

"I think I need to be screaming to get this through your head!"

Morgan's mom stepped forward and shoved Morgan into the wall again.

"Now you listen to me, girl, I'm your mother, I make the decisions, you are in no position to tell me how to live my life! Got that?"

Morgan turned her head away.

"Look at me. Look at me!!"

Morgan turned back.

"I do not want to hear another word- Not one word. I'm dating Kevin, not you, this is my life, not yours."

Morgan thought to herself, "You seem to want to ruin mine, you rule mine, so technically I am dating Kevin, since he beats me too." but she kept her mouth shut.

"Get in your room."

Morgan turned and left, glaring over her shoulder.

"Fairytale." She repeated, throwing her school books on the floor. She slammed her closet door and threw herself on the bed. Morgan watched the golden moonlight stream into her window. Morgan's chest burned, as if fire was destroying what was left of her dreams.

"Prince Charming is an illusion, a figment of your imagination. You'll never find him, you'll never have him, he isn't real." A voice told her.

"I told you, no one wants you, no one loves you, none of your dreams are real or attainable. You're not kind or agreeable. You're not lovely, you're not nice, how could anyone stand you?"

Morgan shut out the cruel words echoing in her mind.

"My future is so uncertain." She thought.

"I'll never fight……..I'll stay married."

Images of a warm summer night flashed in Morgan's head. She squeezed out a tear.

"How could I ever believe my future would hold something good? How could I think there was a happily ever after?" Morgan hugged her soft, white pillow and sobbed.

"I'm reaching for something that doesn't exist." Morgan's mind wandered to where she was at school.

"Mom hasn't even talked to me about college." She thought.

"The least she could do is mention it."

Morgan's alternate mind shot back at her:

"You can't even make the grade in highschool, how do you expect to make it in a University?"

"Work, hard work."

"You're so lazy you'd quit the first week."

Morgan didn't even know what she wanted to study for in the first place.

"Why do I want to go to a school anyway?" Morgan rolled over and closed her eyes.

"O.K, so I'm never going to marry the man of my dreams, never going to get into a school, never going to be the person I want to be…. So what am I doing here?" Morgan desperately searched her mind. She scrunched her eyes shut and tried to think of what would happen next.

What happened she didn't expect.

> "Faith is daring the soul to go farther than it can see."
>
> *- William Newton Clark*

~ Chapter Twenty-Five ~

"Wise words" Produced by Jennifer Rainey
Woman's Day Magazine
April 15th 2003 66th year 8th issue page 166

~ Chapter Twenty-Five ~

Morgan laid silently trying to think, trying not to cry. Then she heard a faint sound. A harmonious voice echoing from nowhere. Morgan opened her eyes and realized it was the lullaby she had been mysteriously hearing. Morgan got up and crouched at her window. Below was a beautiful light, and within it, a woman with long blonde hair and frail features, walking down the sidewalk. The light reflected as tiny rainbows around Morgan's room as she observed in wonder, this phenomenon. The woman continued out of view and Morgan raced down the hall and through the kitchen.

"Hey!" Mrs. Parker screamed, as Morgan ripped the door open and raced down the stairs. She walked out onto the sidewalk and found nothing around. Everything was dark, everything was quiet. Morgan observed the full moon, but promptly went inside. She was in trouble for leaving anyway, why make it worse and stay longer?

Morgan trudged back in and slammed the door shut.

"What was that?" Her mother questioned.

"Nothing, I thought, um, I saw something."

"Right, whatever, get out of my sight."

Morgan went into her room and stared at some of her schoolwork , but a question vexed Morgan the whole time.

Morgan got up and went into her mothers room. It was modestly furnished and clean, with white walls and a hotel-like bedspread. There were a few pictures of Adam and

Morgan on the south wall.

"Mom?"

Morgan's Mom looked up.

"Where did you learn that lullaby that you used to sing?"

"Which lullaby?" Her mother questioned.

"The eerie one."

"Eerie?"

Morgan nodded expectantly.

"Oh, I learned it from grandma."

Morgan's mom continued folding laundry quietly, so Morgan left.

"Now the real question is where did grandma learn it from?" Morgan pondered.

Really, there were many questions, so this one was just added to the list of questions like "Why?" and "What next?". Morgan's mind challenged her heart to search deeper for the answers, into the dark places, where she couldn't even see.

" Today is the most important day of your life, yesterday no longer belongs to you, tomorrow is but an illusion. "

-Anonymous

~ Chapter Twenty-Six ~

~ Chapter Twenty-Six ~

Winter weather had left and March was rolling by quickly. Morgan's grandmother was in the hospital again, and her mom was on the phone with grandpa.

Morgan tried to understand the one way conversation she was hearing.

"No? Come on dad there.... oh, uh huh, ok."

Morgan shifted on the couch to listen.

"How much?"

"Hmmm..."

"Liver biopsy?"

"Oh God, no. Does she know?"

Morgan's heart thumped irregularly.

"How about me? I don't know!" Morgan thought.

"Yes. I see. I will have to. Ok, love you, bye."

Morgan's mom hung up the phone and walked into the living room.

Her face was blanched white as she sat down.

"Grandma has what is called amyloidosis. She has abnormal bleeding and her organs are failing. Honey, she's dying."

Morgan nodded her head understandingly, but inside, her head was spinning. How?

Why? Her pain pounded her body and bounced around like a pinball machine.

Morgan's mother got up and left.

Morgan covered her face and broke down crying. She let her body shake as she sobbed.

"How could you? Do you hate me? Why? Don't do this to me God, don't do this. I promise I'll change, just let her live."

Morgan opened her eyes. She still didn't know why. She still felt an aching pain knowing her grandmother was dying. Nothing would change that.

Morgan's mom contacted work and announced she was picking Adam up from pre-school. Morgan nodded and watched the sun move in and out of the clouds.

Her thin face soaked in the radiant beams as a tear trickled down her cheek.

"I would take her place if I could," Morgan thought.

She almost begged to, but it meant nothing. To her, God wasn't listening; He was too busy flooding a rain forest or something. Morgan laid down and tried to sleep.

This was like a dream, or an alternate reality to her. She would try to dream it away.

Morgan knew she was in a dream now.

She was standing at the foot of her grandmother's hospital bed. Morgan could hear her shallow breathing.

"My child, the time has come," Morgan heard her say.

"Time for what?" Morgan asked puzzled.

Suddenly she sat up, but it wasn't her. A demon-like creature had taken her face. It had gray bubbly skin and gruesome facial features. Its eyes were red and glowing.

"Time for you to see," it quickly replied.

Then Morgan awoke.

Her mom was calling her saying, "Come on Morgan, the car is running!"

Morgan dreaded having to go.

Possibilities of what might happen when she went to see her grandmother invaded her head. Morgan slowly rose and walked out the door and down the steps into the car.

"This may be the last time we see her," Morgan's mom warned.

Morgan nodded, wishing that it weren't true.

Morgan walked up to the hospital room door with her mom and brother.

Morgan stayed with grandpa while mom and Adam went in.

They stayed for about a half hour.

"Why is she... um, dying?" Morgan asked.

Her grandfather turned to face Morgan.

"A secondary problem has occurred, one that is caused by cancer. If they treated it, still, she would only live a year, but now that her organs are shutting down..."

He trailed off, appearing to be thinking of another world.

Morgan lowered her head.

"I remember our first date," grandpa began.

"Your grandmother was so stunning. She wore a yellow chiffon dress with a yellow rose on the front." Morgan's grandfather talked quickly in excitement.

"She had her hair in long ringlets, all pinned up. I told her, 'You look lovely,' and she replied, 'Lovely as what?'" He laughed to himself and stroked his whiskers thoughtfully.

"I always told her I'd find an answer to that question. So the day I proposed, I figured it all out."

Morgan smiled recalling the enchanting story.

"I knelt down on my knee, out in the park, in the rain. Oh, it was so rainy."

Morgan closed her eyes and imagined the quiet rumbles and pitter-pattering of the droplets.

"I got the ring and said, 'You look lovely, lovely enough to be my wife.'"

Morgan's grandpa sighed.

"She never lost her mystery, we never fell out of love, and she never, ever ceased to amaze me. That is true loveliness."

A tear ran down his worn cheek as he spoke.

"Morgan," he said, taking her hand.

"Never settle for less, find a man that will always treasure your beauty and want to take care of you, no matter what."

Morgan nodded.

"Find that special someone who makes you feel special in return. You may go through hard times, yes, but they are worth the rewards. Marriage is work, but if you look at it the right way, it is a lot of fun."

Morgan smiled reflectfully.

"What a pretty girl," grandpa said crying.

"Don't you forget that!"

He snuggled Morgan against his chest as she hung limp in his arms.

"God, I'll miss her," he sobbed.

"Morgan," her mother called.

Her voice was frail and shaking.

"You need to go see her."

Morgan squeezed her grandpa's hand and stepped into the room.

The light from the window streamed in, making everything glittery and bright.

Morgan looked into the bed in front of her. The tiny woman in it was a bluish color, and very thin. She had a beeping machine and bags of fluid beside her. A tube of oxygen was being supplied. Morgan's grandmother slowly lifted her thin arm, offering the chair beside the bed.

Morgan sat down and closed her eyes so she didn't have to look at the grotesque sight in front of her.

Morgan felt her grandmother's cold hand grip hers as she let her tears trickle down her neck.

"My child…"

Morgan looked up in utter disbelief, but was relieved to find it was still her grandmother.

"The time has come."

"Time for what?" Morgan asked cautiously.

"For me to go. For me to meet my Heavenly Father."

Morgan sniffled a bit.

Morgan's grandmother flinched in pain and continued.

"It's time for you to see."

Morgan's grandmother paused from exhaustion.

"To see, that all you have been through is like a stairway being built."

"Built for what?" Morgan questioned.

"For a better life."

Morgan cried harder as her grandma closed her eyes.

"No, no, grandma."

"What dear?"

Morgan heard her lungs gurgle as she breathed.

"What is the lullaby?"

Her grandma smiled broadly, then gripped Morgan's hand tighter as she leaned in and whispered, "Your destiny…"

Morgan closed her eyes and realized what it meant.

God was calling her; she just wasn't listening to Him. He used the music to make her realize He was beckoning her. The music was her destiny laid in His hands.

Morgan felt her grandmother's hand loosen and fall limp.

Morgan looked up to see her eyes closed, and a smile on her face.

Then the machine flat lined.

She was dead.

Nurses rushed in with grandpa at their heels.

"She's a DNR, DNR… please go."

The nurses turned away as Morgan's grandpa knelt next to the bed.

"Isn't she lovely?" he whispered.

"Yes, the loveliest, lovely enough to be an angel."

"We don't see things as they are, we see things as we are."

-Anais Nin

~ Chapter Twenty-Seven ~

~ Chapter Twenty-Seven ~

Morgan watched the nurses turn the machines off and unplug them, turn the sheets over on top of her grandmother's face, over and over in her head.

Morgan decided to skip school all that week. Morgan looked up at the clock and read 10:16 am out loud. She flipped her covers over and walked into the kitchen. She ate some cold pizza, then after a few bites, threw it out.

Morgan paced the kitchen floor at least a dozen times.

She was home alone, hurting, sad, abandoned. None of her friends called, no one cared. Morgan slid down the refrigerator door and stared at the pattern on the floor.

"What am I supposed to do? I can't 'take action', God, what am I to do? I need direction!"

Morgan sat on the cold vinyl floor for hours.

"Why should I continue, I have no reason to live. I have no family, friends, no love and nothing here is worth staying around for."

Morgan considered her grandfather.

"He'll die in a year from loneliness," Morgan stated coldly.

"Adam, what about Adam?" Mia's voice chastised her.

"What about him?" she replied sarcastically.

Morgan was compelled to hurt herself, she hated herself. Hate wasn't even the right word; she loathed, despised, and found herself and her whole life repulsive.

"Why would anyone want me around? I don't anymore."

Morgan walked into the bathroom in a trance.

She opened the medicine cabinet and pulled out a bottle of aspirin.

Morgan's temples were dripping with sweat as she opened the bottle. She poured a glass of water and sat down on the cold tile. She placed the bottle on the floor and laid her head down, staring at the aspirin in front of her.

Morgan's stomach ached and a voice in her head was saying "No!".

Morgan sat up and opened the bottle, tipped it, and poured out a handful of capsules.

Grief pummeled every inch of Morgan's soul.

"I miss her so much."

Morgan thought, rolling the pills in her hand. Her heart shook her chest like it was in a prison cell. Tears welled up in her eyes. She blinked, letting the full, rounded drops fall on her knee.

"Please God, I don't want to do this."

Morgan sat still and collected herself, remembering why she was doing this.

"No one loves me, no one cares, no one is out there, no one understands."

"Why should I continue? I'm worthless now. I've got nothing left in me, nothing left to give."

A voice boomed in her head saying, "You're only worth what you appear to be."

Morgan dumped a few pills in her mouth and swallowed.

Then repeated it.

Morgan took a deep breath and continued pouring aspirin into her hand and swallowing them until her stomach sloshed with water. She looked up to see the time, it was only 2:30, so she laid her head back down on the bathroom floor and cried. This was her end; this is how she would die.

She chose to die this way.

Morgan's stomach felt like it was in a knot. She turned over to feel more comfortable. Her head pounded and she felt hot. Morgan got up to open the window and felt nauseated.

Her stomach beat inside and her mouth tasted dry.

Morgan bent over the toilet rapidly. She felt like she had just run a marathon. Morgan watched sweat soak her clothes as she felt it harder to breathe.

Morgan became scared.

"I don't want to die," she declared in a panic.

Morgan tried to get up, but managed to vomit all over herself.

She fell over and collapsed on the floor. Morgan felt so tired; she probably couldn't even dial 9-1-1.

Then Morgan's mom came home.

Everything was quiet… strangely silent. Mrs. Parker let Adam go into the living room and watch TV and she slowly walked down the hall.

"Morgan? Morgan, where are you?"

Then in horror, she saw Morgan's arm on the bathroom threshold. She raced over and found Morgan unconscious on the floor, covered in vomit.

An empty glass of water and a bottle of aspirin lay on the tiles, spilled over. She grabbed the aspirin bottle and checked its contents, then checked Morgan's pulse.

"Oh my God!" she cried out, feeling her temperature.

"Oh my God!" she repeated.

Morgan's mother raced to the phone and dialed 9-1-1 and asked for an ambulance.

Then she called Kevin.

"Kev, get over here, I need you to take Adam, Morgan has tried to commit suicide!"

The ambulance arrived and they came up the stairs with a stretcher.

One of the EMT's bent over Morgan as she began to have a seizure.

Kevin arrived and the three followed the ambulance in their car.

Morgan remembered being wheeled in on a stretcher, doctors talking and her mother crying.

Then someone said, "Ma'am, your daughter will be fine..."

Morgan woke up in a large hospital room and sunlight pouring in the window.

A lark was outside singing.

Morgan looked over to see an IV bag hanging off a hook and her mother sleeping in a chair.

"Mom?" she breathed out.

Morgan's mom looked over and rushed to her side.

"Oh, Morgan, baby."

Morgan closed her eyes and let tears trickle down her face.

"Honey, why? Why would you do this to yourself?"

Morgan scanned the room with her eyes and let them rest on Kevin, who was standing with his arms crossed in a dark corner.

Morgan's mother followed her eyes.

A look of disappointment crossed her face, and deep lines bordered her mouth.

"Because I'm tired of living like this," Morgan answered.

"I'm tired of being so worn out, worried, tense. I'm tired of looking out for everyone else when no one will look out for me. No one cares about me."

"Morgan, don't say that, please!" Morgan's mother begged.

"That's how I feel," Morgan returned and rolled over, ending the conversation.

Morgan's mom sat back in her chair, frustrated.

"I feel so burdened, Morgan," she stated.

"Now you know how it feels."

"How what feels?"

"To sit and watch someone close to you get hurt and be unable to do anything about it!"

Morgan raised her voice a little, to get her point across.

"I'm sorry, what can I do?" Morgan's mom asked.

Morgan turned over and looked directly into her mother's eyes.

"Get rid of him," Morgan stated flatly, letting her eyes fix onto Kevin.

Morgan's mom was torn. She couldn't lose her daughter over a relationship, and she didn't want to lose a relationship over her daughter.

"I think you're tired, and you need to think about what you're saying," she finally replied.

"No, I think you need to think about what I've said," Morgan returned.

Her mom nodded and got her handbag.

"I'll be back later."

She took Adam by the hand and gestured to Kevin that they leave.

Morgan felt like she was getting ripped from her family.

"How rash could I be?!" she chastised herself.

Kevin stepped over to her bed and leaned in.

"You can't lie forever, Morgan."

Morgan glared at him.

"The person who needs to go here is you, and you know it," Kevin said, stepping back and putting a fake smile on.

"Get well soon!" he shouted so Mrs. Parker could hear, then they left.

Morgan was alone, again. No one cared, she was right. Kevin had no problem telling her so. Her mother communicated it through her regret to leave Kevin because it would make Morgan happy.

"I want grandma back," Morgan thought.

"No one knew me better."

Morgan watched the sun move all day until it got dark, and her family didn't return.

Morgan laid in her hospital bed, fretting over it all night.

"Why do they neglect me? What did I do to deserve this treatment? Why am I so hated?"

The sun rose high and shone in through her window as a doctor stepped in.

"Hello, I'm Doctor Sheridan."

Morgan stared at him defiantly.

"I'm a psychiatrist, I'd like to get to know you, understand you."

"There's nothing to understand," Morgan replied.

"Why is that?" he asked, writing something down.

Morgan rolled her eyes.

"My family hates me and I'm tired of it, that's it, nothing more, nothing less."

"Are you sure?" the doctor prodded.

Morgan thought to herself, "No," but didn't say it.

"Yes."

"Then how does that make you feel?"

"Worthless. How does that make you feel?" Morgan returned sarcastically.

"I can see you're real stressed right now, I'll come back later, how does that sound?"

"Like crap," Morgan replied, turning her head.

The doctor left and Morgan resumed her comfortable position.

"Now I've lost my concentration and I don't know what I was thinking," Morgan said, frustrated.

She laughed to herself, and said out loud in a mocking tone, "How does that make you feel? Ah yes, I am an idiot, good point."

Morgan threw her covers back and wheeled her IV over with her to the window. She looked down and saw the busy street below.

"I wonder if grandma sees things this way," she contemplated.

Morgan observed the cars and how they moved and intertwined on the roads.

She sat down on the radiator and sighed.

"I've got no where to go from here, I guess it's back to agony and pain, the way life is."

"What seems like courage is really persistence- The ability to put part of yourself on hold- Patience."

-Barbara Gordon

~ Chapter Twenty-Eight ~

~ Chapter Twenty-Eight ~

Morgan let the phone ring twelve times, Mia didn't pick up. She called Angela, she didn't pick up. No one wanted to know she was home; no one wanted to see how she was.

The doorbell rang and Morgan put down the phone to answer it.

"Grandpa!" Morgan yelled, hugging him.

He had a lawyer with him.

"Hey dad." Morgan's mom came in.

"This is Mr. Walker, he'll be reading Beatrice's will."

Morgan didn't know this was taking place today.

Everyone sat down as the lawyer explained how her will was legally obtained and witnessed and everything was certified and approved.

"To my husband, Frank Thompson, I leave custody of my personal belongings and stocks, as stated in the adjoining slip."

The lawyer turned the page.

"I also leave my antique jewelry to my daughter, Sarah Thompson-Parker, and my valuable rings."

Morgan's mother sighed and dabbed her eyes with a tissue.

"I leave $5,000 toward my grandson, Adam Parker's college education, to be released to him when he is eighteen."

While Mr. Walker explained, Morgan sat white-knuckled.

"Why didn't she reserve that money for my college? She didn't think I would go to school?"

Morgan's mind spoke,

"You said yourself, you weren't going."

Morgan shut up and listened as the lawyer continued.

"To my granddaughter…"

Morgan leaned in expectantly.

"Morgan Ann Parker, I leave my most prized childhood belongings: a locked book and key, and my favorite dress, I also leave her my wedding dress and dried bouquet."

Morgan was stunned. A wedding dress.

She was certain Morgan was going to get married!

Warmness filled Morgan and a light smile could be traced on her face.

"To my estranged sister, I leave my diamond ring. Anything unmentioned shall be granted to my husband."

Morgan sat silently as her mother signed papers and talked.

She was in deep thought about what just happened.

"In haste I turned to anger because Adam got money, when I got a wedding dress and sentimental things from her childhood. How could I be so selfish?"

The lawyer left and grandpa stayed for dinner.

"That stuff should be looked over and approved for arrival by the end of the month," grandpa said solemnly.

Morgan observed how sad he looked. She was worried for him, hoping she wasn't right thinking he would die too.

Morgan rose from the table and tried calling Mia again. She went into her room and closed the door.

"Hello?"

"Mia, it's Morgan."

"Hi Morgan."

Morgan searched for words uncomfortably, but decided it was no use to be polite, she had been friends with Mia for nine years, nothing could stop that.

"Listen Mia, I know you guys are avoiding me because of what I did, but you don't know everything that has happened here, I haven't been honest."

"I feel sorry for you Morgan, I really do, but you pushed us away. What am I supposed to do?"

"Nothing, I didn't expect you to, I just need a little support right now."

Morgan could hear Mia shift uncomfortably.

Morgan continued.

"My mom's boyfriend, Kevin, has been physically abusing us, and my mom won't let me do anything about it. So that's part of the reason I've been so cold."

Mia was silent.

Morgan's rage built up and she couldn't handle Mia's silence.

She hung up and slammed the phone down onto the floor.

"Thanks a lot Mia," Morgan sobbed.

She curled up in a ball and closed her eyes.

She felt like a bird trapped in a cage.

She had no one to go to, nowhere to turn, no way to explode.

She was a ticking bomb, who would take out the whole block once time ran out.

"There is no remedy for love, but to love more."

- Henry David Thoreau

~ Chapter Twenty-Nine ~

Taken from "The Second Summer of the Sisterhood" by Ann Brashares. Delacorte Press- an imprint of Random House Children's Books, a division of Random House, Inc.

Used with permission.

~ Chapter Twenty-Nine ~

S ummer broke through and rested satisfied in late May. Morgan thought it would never come. She was tired of seeing Mia, Angela, and Ryan at school and not being able to talk to them.

Morgan stepped out on the roof. The wind whisked her hair over her dark green eyes and made her baggy pants rumple in the breeze. She took a breath and let her spirit soar. This was the only way she found rest. The rooftop, the skyline; that was her sanctuary.

Morgan never dared to open the three boxes left to her from her grandma. They reminded her too much of the pain and suffering that went along with her death.

Though it had only been two months, Morgan thought her heart was healed; really, she had no heart to heal anymore.

She stored her heart on the rooftop, and only took it out when she was up there, alone and able to be herself.

Morgan went back downstairs and into her apartment. She sat down on the toilet seat and read the directions to the hair dying kit she bought. Morgan got up and stared at herself in the mirror. Black. Black hair would suit her pale features and thin face.

She ripped open the box and put on the gloves; she squeezed the mixed formula onto her head and swirled it around into every strand. Morgan wrapped her hair in a towel and counted how long to keep it in for.

Morgan went into her bedroom and walked over to her jewelry box. She pulled out the locket her father gave her that past Christmas. It glittered and shined. Morgan rubbed the smooth surface and held it up.

"I can wear this as a necklace," Morgan observed.

She fished through the drawer for a matching silver chain.

Morgan stopped searching and pulled out a long rope-like chain. It was delicate and ornamental in its intricate design. Morgan sat on the bed as she let her eyes rest on it for a long time.

"This is the chain grandma gave me." Morgan closed her eyes and brought it close to her chest.

"She touched this, thought about this, for me. She thought about me when she got this."

Morgan squeezed her eyes shut and envisioned her grandmother's shining smile.

"The only way you are going to heal is if you embrace your loss," Morgan could hear her therapist saying.

Morgan rolled her eyes and put the locket onto the necklace.

She clasped it around her neck and let the chain fall down past her black shirts' neckline.

She stretched the collar down to observe how it rested. It laid comfortably on her bare skin, over the place where her real heart was stored. Morgan tucked it under her shirt, concealed, and went back into the bathroom and rinsed her hair out.

Her long locks had grown since last year and now fell down around her waist.

Morgan blow dried it and examined her dark hair in the mirror.

"I almost look like Angela, minus the purple hair."

Angela had a short bobbed cut anyway.

Plus Morgan's build was much smaller, but she enjoyed bingeing on chocolate since her near death experience, so she gained about ten pounds, weighing near 120 pounds now.

She went into her room and continued to observe her reflection in her mirror.

Morgan stepped back, tripping on the boxes of inherited goods. Morgan tried to find something sturdy to grip, but accidentally grabbed the mat on her dresser, causing everything to fall off onto her head.

Morgan plopped onto the boxes, which now were crushed from her sitting on them.

"Grr, why am I so clumsy?" Morgan complained, taking the stuff out of her lap.

Then she heard a song playing.

Morgan's heart raced and her eyes scanned the floor for the source of the song.

It was the old music box. From the fall, it started up, revealing its mysterious tune- the lullaby.

Morgan crawled over, and turned the music box over, so it sat upright on the floor.

"This was grandma's music box, which mom had to have heard, or grandma sang to her, so that's how I knew it."

Morgan let the song unwind until it slowed to a complete silence. She could hear the traffic outside and felt the pounding of a bass line playing from another apartment.

Morgan picked the box up and placed everything back in its spot on the dresser with the music box.

She stood reticent for several minutes before regaining her composure.

"This song has been haunting me for more than a year and it was in my room all along!"

Then Morgan heard her mother's footsteps in the kitchen, talking to Kevin.

Morgan waltzed in, trying to flaunt her new hair color.

"Morgan, what did you do to your hair?"

"I colored it."

"It looks awful," Kevin added.

"No, no, I think it looks fine, but you should have asked, Morgan!"

"You would have said no, so I just had to prove to you it looks good before you go and judge on something you haven't even seen."

"Ok, whatever," her mother replied, turning and putting her purse on the kitchen table.

"Looks good?!" Kevin bellowed.

"Yes Kevin, I have no problem with it."

"So you're going to let your brat teenager rebel, and then tell her that her disobedience was a good idea?"

"I never told her no, besides Kevin, she has to make her own choices now."

Morgan beamed.

"No Sarah, she's washing it out."

"Kevin, she's NOT your daughter."

"Well, she needs a father!" Kevin boomed.

"And you're not qualified!" Morgan's mom screamed, getting in his face.

Kevin slapped her cheek, and glared into her eyes.

"We're over, Kevin, goodbye."

"Excuse me?" Kevin asked, shocked.

"I hate you, I don't know why I even went out with you, get out."

"Oh my God, you'll be sorry, very sorry if you don't…"

Mrs. Parker cut him off.

"Get out or I will report you!"

Kevin's anger turned into fear as he backed away.

"Fine, but I'll be back, to get some stuff."

"You don't have anything here, and if you do, I'll mail it to you!

Goodbye!"

Morgan's mom slammed the door and locked it.

"That felt good!" she declared.

"See mom, I told you."

"Don't even go there, you're the last person who should be giving out self-respect speeches."

Morgan's lip quivered in disapproval. She fought back the tears, which caused her throat to tense up.

"I...I, I don't know what to say..."

"I thought you were just, just being blinded. Now I see that I am. You do hate me."

"Morgan," her mother called as Morgan burst out the door and down the street.

She unlocked her bike from the parking meter at her side and pedaled away.

"Morgan!"

Her mother chased down the sidewalk after her as tears ran down her face. The hurt was unfathomable. No one could understand her pain. She had to go somewhere no one would find her, so she raced as far as her feet could push her. She crashed her bike at the first light post of the Brooklyn Bridge and she ran to the center. Morgan collapsed onto the sidewalk and looked up at the stormy clouds brewing a thunderstorm above her.

Morgan closed her eyes and listened to the raging river below as the winds picked up and a streak of lightning scored the sky.

Then rain began to fall, hard.

Morgan meditated on the pounding of the bridge from cars going over the seams.

"Mom won't figure I'm here at all," she guessed.

"No one will, I can just disappear."

Morgan's mind raced and her clothes were drenched by the pouring rain.

Morgan stood up and took hold of a Jersey barrier for stability.

She gripped the rail and looked down at the river, she would try again, this time she wouldn't fail.

"Summer afternoon, summer afternoon; to me, those have always been the most beautiful words in the English language."

-Henry James

~ Chapter Thirty ~

~ Chapter Thirty ~

Morgan stepped away from the railing and flopped herself back onto the concrete.

"What am I doing?" Morgan asked.

She looked down at her watch and found it was after 4:00 p.m. She sat for an hour and just watched the traffic pass by. Then the rain stopped and the sun came out.

Morgan got up to leave, but couldn't bring herself to walk back to her bike and ride home. Her mom would be there, waiting. She was tired of going back home after she had left it so many times. She had run away from it to escape, now would she deliver herself into its grasp?

Morgan inhaled the deeply refreshing scent of rain and diesel fuel.

Tomorrow was the first day of June, the anniversary of the day her dad left.

Now, the day she had too.

Morgan turned around and faced the railing. She knew what she had to do. She placed her foot into the scrollwork and grabbed a hold of a pole. Then she lifted herself onto the top of the frame and looked out over all of the river as the sun set. Morgan closed her eyes and let go of the pole. She let her arms fly outward as if she were flying. A broad grin stretched across her face.

"God," she called out.

"I hear you! I understand now, that I can't do this on my own. I see that I'm not here to live my life for me. I can't reach my life goals by myself. I need you, I need to reach for you, to accomplish my goals."

Morgan felt a raindrop fall on her nose and the heavens opened up and tears came falling from the sky.

"I need to go back to start! Please God, Jesus, show me how! I need to know why I'm here, show me, give me a sign, so I know how to live for you!"

Morgan heard someone behind her.

Then she heard someone speak.

"Ya know, someone once said, 'God isn't the starting point, He's the very force that drives the point,' the point of life."

Morgan put her hands down and carefully looked behind her.

It was Mia.

"Won't you come down and talk?"

"Ok."

"Your mom told me what happened, let's go for a walk."

"Ok."

Morgan jumped back onto the sidewalk and scooped up Mia's hand.

"Morgan, you know I love you, and my weakness is not knowing how to show you my love."

Morgan watched Mia's feet as she walked.

"But God said to us that his love is deeper than the oceans, that's one huge display of love!"

Mia giggled.

Morgan smiled out of reflex.

"You can't find the answer in yourself, you need to look deep in your heart, you need to find Jesus."

"Mia, I'm afraid I don't know where my heart is! I've lost it," Morgan complained.

"Christ has already taken care of that, you don't need to worry about 'losing your heart.' He holds it."

Morgan let the salty tears run down her face.

"Your purpose is in Christ, and in you is Christ. You've been running from what you have searched for your whole life!"

Morgan let go and sobbed at the utter relief the truth brought to her weary soul. She had found her answers.

Why? For God.

What next? Soul search, for Jesus.

How? Already taken care of.

"Youth group is tonight, actually, it's in an hour. Angela and Ryan are going."

Morgan thought hard.

"It will answer so many of your questions if you'd just listen to what you hear."

Morgan decided this was the breaking point.

"I don't remember ever saying this to myself, 'This is my breaking point,' so I guess I've reached my end."

Mia's eyes grew large and she turned and took Morgan's shoulders in her hands.

"That's the beauty of it! God is the point- your breaking point, your end- His beginning!"

"We are born not once, but again and again."

-William Charles

~ Chapter Thirty-One ~

~ Chapter Thirty-One ~

Morgan slowly walked into the youth room, wiping her face clean of all tears.

Teens like her were standing around, talking, some were playing air hockey on the game table in the corner, and some others were seated, eating popcorn available at the round tables. Mia guided Morgan over to the table where Angela and Ryan sat.

Angela turned and looked at Morgan in surprise.

"Morgan! I've been praying for you for weeks! I'm so glad you're here!"

"Thanks," Morgan said, smiling.

"Have a good time," Ryan said.

"I like your hair," Angela laughed.

Morgan gripped her wet stringy hair strands.

She had forgotten they were black. Morgan laughed loudly when she noticed Angela's pink hair now was green.

"I love your lawn, Angela!" she teased.

The four sat down and talked while Morgan piled popcorn into her mouth.

"Alright people! Quiet down, take a seat!" the youth pastor announced.

Morgan observed his look.

He had dark brown hair, cut short, but brought up to small points. He had a medium build and looked very active.

His eyes looked kind and wise.

Morgan looked closer at his face.

He had a straight nose and all his features were even and proportionate. In his hands he held a worn Bible and had some crinkled papers shoved inside. The room quieted down and he began to speak.

Ryan leaned over and whispered to Morgan.

"That's Pastor James, Jay for short."

Morgan nodded in acknowledgement.

"Tonight we are going to cover a small piece on love. The first in our four-week study. Tonight we will discuss how our Lord is love, and how love came to be."

Jay opened his Bible and declared it was time to pray.

Morgan's hands were sweaty and she felt like Jell-O. She concentrated hard on not looking around the room.

"God, help me lose myself, so I can find you, help me clear away the shattered pieces of my life that clutter any way to you," Morgan begged.

Then she looked up as Pastor Jay began the lesson.

"Romans 12:9 through 12 says, "Let love be without hypocrisy. Abhor what is evil. Cling to what is good. Be kindly affectionate to one another with brotherly love, in honor giving reference to one another' not lagging in diligence, fervent in spirit, serving the Lord; rejoicing in hope, patient in tribulation, continuing steadfastly in prayer."

People all around Morgan were reading along with open Bibles. She didn't have hers; it was at home, crammed on a shelf.

"So let's take some key words from this verse; one would be 'brotherly.' Brotherly love means 'like family,' love everyone like they were part of your family. Now I know not all of us love our family at times."

Morgan chuckled to herself.

"But that's where the next word comes in," the youth pastor continued.

"With honor, love them with honor. This can also be translated as 'respect.' So love everyone with respect, as if they were a part of your family.

Next, 'be fervent in spirit.' Does anyone know what that could mean?"

A couple of people called out some definitions, but Morgan kept silent.

"It means to keep growing in Christ. If you love Him, you will be able to love others through Him, by Him, the way God loves every one of us."

Morgan didn't believe God could love her, but she kept open. Since she was trying to lose that attitude, she shut it out and concentrated on understanding the message.

"In Genesis 2:18, God invented love for man, saying, "It is not good that man should be alone," so God made Adam a wife, a wife he could love.

Morgan kicked the image of her brother naked in the woods out of her head.

"God is the inventor of love, people! If you think you'll never find love, or God doesn't love you, than you're wrong! God is incapable of not loving you, of not giving you someone to love and to love you. If you're feeling that way, it's because you're not loving yourself, in that case, you're missing something important in your life."

"What is it? What am I missing?" Morgan asked in her head.

"Tell me! Tell me! You're talking about me, I have to find out what I'm missing."

"1st Corinthians 13:4-8 explains what real love is: patient, kind, humble, doesn't envy, not prideful, not rude or selfish, not angered and is never wrong or evil. It is truthful, protects, trusts, hopes, and perseveres. And here's the cherry on top: love never, never... fails."

Morgan leaned back in her chair.

"Love is so much. I have never had love! I have never felt or given this."

"So as I close, let me quote the book of Jeremiah."

Jay turned the pages of his Bible and paused, taking a deep breath.

"For I know the thoughts that I think toward you, says the Lord, thoughts of peace and not of evil, to give you a future and a hope. Then you will call upon me and go and pray to me, and I will listen to you."

Morgan's heart raced faster.

"Where was this all through my troubles?"

Morgan's motherly voice answered.

"Hidden on a shelf, neglected, in your Bible."

Morgan let a tear drop from her face.

The pastor continued enthusiastically.

"And you will seek me, and find me with all your heart. I will be found by you, says the Lord. I will bring you back from your captivity..."

Morgan closed her eyes and wept.

God was there, He did hear her, because He did love her, He was listening.

Never in her wildest dreams did Morgan imagine this could happen to her.

She was vulnerable and embarrassed, crying in public. She was cold and wet and dying on the inside, but a light had broken through, causing her to want to go a step further into that vulnerable place.

"So if any of you are feeling alone tonight, if you're getting the idea that you're missing something, you're in luck! There is an answer to that burning question, and it all starts with Him."

The youth pastor pointed upwards to the vaulted ceiling.

"Your life is not about how you can use God to lessen your burdens, or to make a situation work, it's about how He can use you for His purpose."

Morgan stared in wonder as the youth pastor met her eyes.

"You are not worthless. You are God's precious child."

Morgan let out an involuntary cry as Mia pulled her close and held her head.

"If you're willing to make a step tonight, let's close with this prayer. Jesus, thank you for loving me, even though I didn't understand what love was or why it was. You stayed with me, showing your love for me…"

Morgan repeated the words in her heart, wailing out loud, as tears soaked her thankful face.

"Thank you for showing me how much you loved me, dying on the cross for me. I accept that sacrifice, come into my life, and grow in me. Change my life, so you can use me. Forgive me and purify me, I know any sin is not beyond forgiveness. I believe you died on the cross, took my sins, and rose from the dead three days later. You saved me from my fate and I believe I will go to heaven with you forever. Until then, guide me, plant me, grow me, and mold me. Fill me with your Holy Spirit so I may show your love, the way you show love, to others, until you return and take me away. Give me power to stand for your truth tonight and develop as a Christian, following your love. My love for you overflows God, I love you first, in Jesus name, Amen."

Morgan didn't open her eyes; she sat in her chair, shaking as tears fell from her chin.

"If you prayed that prayer, please let me know…"

Morgan immediately raised her hand as high as it could go, as if she were attempting to touch God's face, which she felt she had.

Everyone stood and sang the closing song;

Morgan couldn't stand. She fell onto the hard, blue carpet and cried out.

When the song faded, she laid still as a song came into her head.

She sang "Amazing Grace" out loud as everyone else joined her.

She took back everything she had ever said, anything she had ever done. She was new; she was born again.

"What is that you express in your eyes? It seems to me, more than all the words I have ever read in my life. "

-*Walt Whitman*

~ Chapter Thirty-Two ~

Taken from "The Second Summer of the Sisterhood" by Ann Brashares. Delacorte Press- an imprint of Random House Children's Books, a division of Random House, Inc. Used with permission.

~ Chapter Thirty-Two ~

Morgan slept soundly that night and felt rested in the morning.

"Morgan," her mom began as she poured her cereal.

"I'm sorry about my offensive words yesterday, obviously they hurt you."

"I understand mom. I forgive you," Morgan said, looking up at her, smiling.

"What happened to you while you were out?" her mother asked, mystified.

"God, amazing…"

Morgan choked up due to her lack of words. She was unable to express her joy.

Her mom stared at her for a long time before returning to her bowl.

Adam crawled onto his chair and poured his cereal happily.

Morgan walked by to get her spoon and ruffled his long messy hair.

Mrs. Parker glanced up again in wonder.

Then the doorbell rang.

Morgan's mom jumped up and looked through the peephole.

"It's probably Ke…"

She stopped speaking and called Morgan over.

"Morgan, do you know who this is?"

Morgan glanced through the hole.

"Hey, that's Pastor Jay, the youth pastor."

"Oh," Morgan's mom said, unlocking the door.

Morgan stepped forward to greet him.

"Hey, Morgan?" he asked.

"Yes, um, this is my mom."

Mrs. Parker stared into his deep blue eyes in wonder.

"Wow, um, hi, I'm Sarah, Morgan's mom, uh, you already knew that…" she tapered off.

"Want to come in?" Morgan offered.

"Sure, hey, listen, your friend, Mia, gave me your address so I could come and talk to you. She told me about some of your struggles."

Morgan hoped this wouldn't turn into a psyc session.

Morgan's mother continued to gaze at Jay admiringly.

"I saw you last night and something told me you needed to hear that."

Morgan fought back the emotions.

"Yes I did," she squeaked.

"He told me to say that, to say 'you're not worthless'."

Morgan's dam broke and tears drenched her face.

"I would like to hear about your life, if that's ok."

Morgan's mom rose.

"I'll leave you guys in private."

"Thank you Sarah."

Morgan's mother blushed and shuffled out of the kitchen.

Morgan started all the way back to that warm June night when she was twelve. She told Jay about her struggles in school, with Jared and Kevin. The abuse hate they expressed toward her.

She explained in great detail about her relationship with Mike Miganouski and her grandmother's death.

She felt comfortable telling him, but with the therapists and psychiatrists, she hated talking. Something in Jay's eyes made her feel at ease.

Morgan didn't tell him about the music box until after; she really didn't want to share that, but it was a vital part of her life story.

"You know what you call that? An unbelievably moving testimony!" James yelled enthusiastically.

"Yeah, I know."

"Ya know what I think? You need to open the boxes your grandmother left you."

"Why?"

"Well, this book, it sounds like a big deal, it has a key, so it locks. What book locks unless it is absolutely personal?"

"Like a diary…" Morgan thought out loud.

"Your grandmother sounds like she was an outstanding Christian; if it is a journal, she wanted you to read it, and grow from it."

"You're right, Jay, I should look at it."

"Hey, I've got to go now, but if you'd like, I'd love to bring you and your mom to lunch sometime."

"Me too?" Adam squealed.

"Sure buddy."

Morgan smiled warmly. Jay was a great guy. She really liked being around him.

The youth pastor rose to leave and said goodbye to Morgan and Adam as her mom came in.

Mrs. Parker fell all over herself as he left.

"Wow, now that is a man!" Morgan's mom swooned.

"Mom!" Morgan shrieked.

"What? Isn't he the greatest guy you've seen? In five minutes I feel as if I've known him for ten years!"

Morgan had to agree. He communicated a sense of oneness, of love, brotherly love.

"Whew, he really does live what he preaches!"

Morgan's mom went to the stove and started making lunch.

"Morgan, I can't believe he was here for so long!"

"I know!"

"What did you guys talk about?"

Morgan hesitated.

"Um, my life."

"Really?" her mom asked interested.

"Yeah, and about…"

The doorbell rang again.

"For crying out loud!" Morgan's mom fumed.

She walked over to the door and looked through the hole again.

"Oh God, it's Kevin."

Morgan could hear him calling to her from the other side of the door.

"Sarah! You witch! Let me in! I'm not through with you!"

"He's drunk," Morgan's mom stated nervously.

"Take Adam out of here."

"Ok," Morgan agreed and guided Adam into the living room.

The phone rang and Mrs. Parker picked it up.

"Leave me alone!" she screamed, and slammed it back onto the receiver.

"Who was that?" Morgan asked puzzled.

"It's him, on his cell phone!" her mother sniffled.

"Maybe we should call the police now," Morgan suggested.

"He'll know and then he'll just come back tomorrow or next week, or next month."

"What other option do we have? He's a strong, powerful man, and he's drunk, stalking us."

Morgan's mom nodded in agreement while Kevin continued to pound on the door.

"Someone else is going to call the cops at this point."

Mrs. Parker laughed.

"I'll just talk to him through the door, he knows I'm home already, but maybe you should stay out of sight, so he won't know you are too," she whispered.

Morgan moved from the stove, out of the way.

"I'm not going to leave the room, though."

Her mom shook her head understandingly and chained the door up and unlocked the bolts. She slowly pulled it open to the maximum length of the chain.

"Why are ya doin' this, Sarah?"

"I told you, we're over, I'm serious."

"Well, so am I. I'm sorry, ok?"

"Ya know what, Kev? I don't care. Get lost!"

Kevin fumed through the crack.

"Why you…"

He thrust his hand through the open space and grabbed the chain and ripped it down. Morgan's mom screamed and fell backwards. She stood still like a statue, stunned as Kevin walked into the kitchen, throwing the broken hardware on the floor.

He didn't say anything; he just covered his face with his hand while leaning on the table with his other.

"Look what you made me do!" he gestured.

"What I made you do? You're the one with the scotch in your pocket!" Morgan pointed.

"Get out Kevin, I want you to leave, we are over."

Kevin nodded his head and backed out of the apartment.

Morgan's mom shut and locked the door as Kevin swore and kicked the frame with his boot.

"Yikes!" Morgan said, stunned.

"Glad that's over."

"For now," her mom added, picking up tiny screws from the chain lock.

"You should get a restraining order," Morgan suggested.

"What will a stupid piece of paper do, Morgan? Nothing! Nothing at all!" her mom screamed.

"It was only a suggestion, jeeze."

"Forget it," her mom said, throwing a hand towel.

"Oh, so now you're mad at me?"

"No, I have been all along, this is just it. I'm tired of you Morgan,

212

sick and tired of your attitude."

"Well, I've been trying, ok?"

Morgan knew she shouldn't have said that, since this was her first day of 'trying'.

"I would never have known…" her mom sarcastically replied.

Morgan tossed the comment aside.

"Have you ever thought that maybe my problems were from your attitude? The way you treat me? The way you talk to me?"

"What way Morgan, what way?"

"You're always trying to dump responsibility on me, responsibility that you should take. And you're always putting me down now. Why do you think I left yesterday? To get away from you! I can't stand you anymore!"

Morgan closed her mouth. She had gone too far.

Her mom glared at her defiantly.

"You're frustrating me mom, don't you get it?" Morgan finished quietly.

Her mother continued to tap her foot and stare at her with her hands on her hips.

"I guess not."

Morgan slowly turned and went down the hall into her room. She could hear her mother crying over Adam asking her why.

"She won't apologize, so I won't. I just tried to be honest," Morgan convinced herself.

A voice rose up in her head.

"Love is…"

"Grrr…" Morgan huffed, and she went back into the kitchen.

"Mom, I'm sorry. That was stupid of me."

Her mom turned her back and nodded.

"I've only been 'trying' for a day, and apparently, it isn't working."

Morgan's mother chuckled a little, then turned around.

"We've been through a lot. I can understand you're frustrated. I've been taking my own frustration out on you. I'll try to catch myself before I do, from now on."

Morgan nodded her head in approval, grabbed an apple, and went back into her room.

Morgan looked at the imploded boxes on her floor, but cast them aside. She went over to the music box and turned it on.

Morgan went over to her bookshelf and scanned it for a particular book.

She pulled out her Bible and brushed all the dust off.
She sat down on her bed and read for the rest of the afternoon.

"Live your life and forget your age."

-*Norman Vincent Peale*

~ Chapter Thirty-Three ~

~ Chapter Thirty-Three ~

Morgan let her arms hang loosely off her rumpled bed. Today was her 16th birthday, and her party. Morgan rose and got dressed.

She put on a pair of jeans and a loose tank.

She put her hair up in a braided bun and went into the kitchen.

"Our highs for today are record breaking, here's the outline…"

Morgan stared into the TV screen.

"10 am to noon will be 85 degrees, do all your yard work and exercise then. At about 2:00, the temperatures will soar to 102 degrees…"

"Mom!" Morgan screamed.

"It's going to be a hundred today!"

"I know!" her mom called happily from the bathroom doorway.

"At about five pm, we will be watching for thunderstorms to develop as a cold front comes through…"

"We will have to finish the party before then," Morgan's mom decided, walking into the room.

"Mama, I don't like thunderstorms," Adam complained.

"Neither do I," Morgan joined in, teasingly.

Mrs. Parker gave her a warning look, jokingly, then went up onto the roof and set a table with lemonade and some sandwiches. Morgan's friends soon arrived along with Pastor Jay.

Then grandpa, Adam, and mom came up. The sun gladly shone brightly on them.

Mrs. Parker brought the cake over and lit it. Morgan watched her move to every wick. How frail and delicate her hands now were. How age affected her.

Morgan blinked slowly, knowing the time wasn't watching her then.

She turned and watched Adam's little face break into laughter as grandpa tickled his belly.

She watched how when Mia and Ryan were talking, Ryan slipped his fingers smoothly around hers.

Morgan observed everyone, every age. Almost in slow motion, she froze the images in her heart.

Her mother turned and presented the cake. Morgan could hear

her friends and family echoing in the background.

"Time for a wish," Adam shrilled excitedly.

Morgan stared down at the pink sprinkles. She was like a raindrop, delicate and small. Once the rain hit the ground, it was over. Morgan's life was by no means over. She was glad it wasn't. Her wish was to make her life into all it could be, and more. Morgan blew out the candles forcefully.

"Man, it's so hot, I'm surprised those went out!" Angela commented.

Everyone laughed.

Morgan stood up.

"Everybody, I have something to say."

Grandpa quieted Adam and the girls.

Mom stopped cutting the cake.

James stared expectantly.

"I know this past year has been hard, for me especially, but I just wanted to say something, grandma's last words to me were that my hardships were 'building a stairway to a better life' and I accept that. I just wanted you all to know that I appreciate you being here all along, and you're a special part in my life, you always will be."

Grandpa smiled warmly and Angela wiped a tear off of her dark face.

"That was beautiful," she teased.

Ryan shoved a balloon into her hair as Mia and Angela shrieked over the cake in his lap, flopping over onto his pants.

Today Morgan turned 16, but this wasn't even the beginning of her journey.

After the party ended, thunder erupted over the horizon.

Mia stayed and ate leftover pizza with Morgan.

"Today was a good day, huh?"

"Definitely!" Morgan agreed as thunder clapped overhead.

"There's a severe thunderstorm watch out tonight."

"Yeah, I know," Mia acknowledged.

"Maybe I should go home now. I don't want to get stuck in it."

"True," Morgan agreed.

"I'll see you later this week."

"Ok!"

"Happy birthday!" Mia called as she shut the door.

Morgan walked over to her window and waved to Mia below in the pouring rain.

Then suddenly lightning crashed into a transformer and took the power out.

Morgan groped through the darkness to find Adam. She followed his screams into his room.

"Adam, it's ok, the lights went out, that's all."

"Morgie!" he cried.

Morgan went over to the window and found Mia had left safely.

The rain rumbled on the roof as Mrs. Parker passed a flash light to Morgan and Adam.

Morgan left Adam and went into her own room. She felt around for her candles and brought them forward, placing them on the floor. Morgan grabbed a box of matches and lit all three.

"Ma, I've got candles, so I'm going to stick the flashlight in the bathroom to save the battery."

"Ok," she heard her mother answer.

Morgan plunked herself onto the hardwood floor and watched the orange flames flicker.

They lighted the boxes at her side.

Morgan decided to open them up.

She started with the biggest, which held the wedding dress and a bouquet of dried hydrangeas in a glass container, lying delicately on a satin pillow.

She lifted the glass chamber out and pushed the box away from the candles. Morgan gently pulled the gown out and held it up to herself.

The veil laid on the bottom of the box. She stuck it on and examined herself in the mirror.

The dress had long tight sleeves with ruffles at the end of the cuffs.

Up the arms was tightly sewn embroidery. The collar ruffled around her neck and large embroidered flowers made a V down the front. The waist was tight and laced in the back like a corset. The back of the dress hung loosely to the ground with a lightweight lace over it.

Lightning illuminated the room in a foggy haze. Morgan lowered the dress and proceeded to the next box. Inside laid a little girls dress.

It had large short sleeves that poofed at the shoulders.

The neck had a rounded collar and broach. The colors were beige and orange stripes. Little flower petals floated down in the pattern of the vertical stripes.

It had a tie knotted in the back that fell to the lacy trim on the bottom of the dress.

Morgan replaced it in the box and pulled out the smallest box. It was barely big enough to hold a pair of shoes.

Morgan sat down next to the candlelight and peeled back the tape.

Inside laid another box, wrapped in a feminine gift paper, with a card marked 'Morgan' on top.

Morgan lifted the smaller box out and ripped the card open.

Inside it said:

Morgan,

Today is your 16th birthday, how do I know?

That's what I anticipated. I thought you should wait until then to receive this special gift.

To everything, there is a season, and this is your season, my child. Your mother never received this because she was well on her way to becoming a woman by then, and you're my special girl now. I had this present given to me by my mother, and she got it from her grandmother. That's as far as it has been traced. Please accept it in prayer and love.

This is a big step toward your climb to real loveliness, as your grandfather says. God will bless you with this magical book, I'm sure.

> *With all my love,*
> *Grandma.*

Morgan stared at the writing for a long time. Rumbles filled the sky as streaks of light brightened the sky every so often.

"It's her handwriting," Morgan thought.

"There is no way to tell when she wrote this…" Morgan told herself, checking all over the envelope for a clue.

Morgan placed the card onto the dark floor and slowly ripped open the delicate wrapping. After the wrapping was removed, another box was revealed, but this one was decorative. It had a pattern of yellow, orange, and red roses on the sides; the lid was decorated in a pinstripe pattern.

Morgan, in a trans-like state, lifted the lid and found a small book bound across by a small gold band. The book itself was old, but black velvet was discernable. Morgan wiped the dust and dirt off the cover and revealed the writing underneath. The title read:

"Book of Dreams."

Morgan tilted her head in wonder. She turned the book on its side. A tiny pad lock was attached to a loop in the gold band.

A key was not found.

Morgan searched the book carefully, then looked inside the box.

Morgan inspected the floor, in case she had dropped it. Nothing.

"The will said there was a key included!"

Morgan thought hard.

Then an idea popped into her head as she remembered her last conversation with grandma.

"Grandma, what is the lullaby?"

"Your destiny."

Morgan realized her earlier conclusion was that the lullaby song drew her to her destiny, God. So if the lullaby were played to draw her to Him, maybe it would draw the key to her instead.

Morgan wound the music box and let it play over the book.

Suddenly a small sliver of metal sprung from the binding. Morgan put the music box on the floor and examined the metal sticking out. It was an antique key, sprung by the sound of the music.

Morgan smiled in satisfaction.

"I was right!"

Morgan inserted the key into the lock and turned it.

A low click could be heard and the gold rod popped up, giving access to the contents.

Morgan lifted the lid, revealing the true cover of the book.

The velvet was like a kind of slipcover to protect the ancient book.

The cover had a picture of a young woman in a long white robe, glowing features, and fairy-like wings, holding the likeness of the book.

Again, in long scrolling words, the title "Book of Dreams," could be seen on the top. Morgan flipped the cover over to the first page and began to read:

"This is the beginning of your enchanted journey, where many mysteries await you."

Below these words was a small oval frame, with a foggy mirror.

Morgan continued to read the italicized lettering.

"There is a child hidden inside of you; our heart. Look into her eyes, is there happiness? Contentment? In your mirror, do you not see her?"

Morgan gazed into the tiny mirror.

"No, I don't see her," Morgan answered, tapping the glass.

"Is this thing broken?" she asked frustrated.

A jagged streak of lightning flashed and a loud crash followed, sending chills down Morgan's back as she continued.

"She is gone, lost in the cobwebs of a broken dream. She has left. She has been forgotten. You have left behind the enjoyment of fields and dreams, of butterflies and sunny skies."

Morgan could smell the scent of wild flowers and fresh grass.

She shoved her nose in the page and inhaled deeply.

"This book smells like grass..." Morgan commented, bewildered.

"Rediscover the adventure of a prince in armor, dreams of fairies, and visions of beautiful angels."

Morgan slowly turned the page, and found it had a mirror also. Only this one lighted up; fog churned and blew inside it mysteriously.

"Your mind tells you that this is just a book, a story. That it is fake, unreal, untrue. That it is unreachable. It can be true, for you, if you follow your heart. A little girl behind the glass is looking back at you..."

Immediately a girl, similar to the one Morgan had seen in her dream while sleeping on the couch, appeared, she looked straight at Morgan and reached her thin fingers out at her.

Morgan slammed the book shut.

"That is way too creepy!" Morgan yelled, backing away.

Morgan could hear the wind outside howling, and rain and thunder pounded on her window.

She was in a dark room, illuminated by the flicker of three small candles. Morgan thought about her situation.

"Spooky position, spooky book, spooky room..."

Morgan reopened the book to the spot she left off at, and continued reading.

"You have misplaced the looking glass that peers into your soul. All you need is her, the child you have left behind. Many dark secrets and mysteries lie on every page of this book. Adventure is hidden inside of every word. Your logic can't guide you here; your senses can't pull you out. You can't deny your soul's forgotten dreams any longer."

Morgan became alarmed.

Should she continue?

"This sounds like witchcraft!" she thought.

Morgan glanced down to where she left, the last paragraph.

"Unlock your door, unlatch the chamber of your heart, discover a mystical world, where all you must do is dream."

Morgan looked into the small mirror and thought, "I want to dream again."

The fancy words caused the gazing girl in the mirror to fade away, and replaced her.

Morgan leaned in and read them out loud.

"Mirror, mirror, in my heart, I feel I'm falling apart…"

Before she could finish, Morgan felt a strange sensation and realized the book was growing in size. She felt like a character from "Alice and Wonderland"; actually, she felt like Alice as the book grew.

The mirror was nearly life sized as Morgan watched the words dissolve.

The fogginess was now the image as Morgan felt a pulling force coming from the mirror. She tried to grip the pages to resist the suction, but there was no use, she was already in a dream, and in dreams, you don't control what happens to you.

"Not all who wander are lost. "
                              -*J.R.R Tolkien*

~ Chapter Thirty-Four ~

Taken from "The Sisterhood of the Traveling Pants" by Ann Brashares. Delacorte Press- an imprint of Random House Children's Books, a division of Random House, Inc.

~ Chapter Thirty-Four ~

Morgan found herself flat on her face, but what shocked her was that she was not on any surfaces. Morgan jumped up, alarmed by this unnatural suspension.

She looked around and found nothing but blackness. She looked above her and saw a tiny light.

Morgan reached up and carefully pulled it down. It was as small as a grain of sand, yet shone as bright as a million lights. She gazed at it in the palm of her hand when suddenly it vanished, causing small stars to form above, around, and below her.

"Amazing..." she breathed out.

Morgan let her eyes wander over behind her, to where a silver moon hung.

To her disbelief, a beautiful woman was reclined on it. The folds of her robe held millions of stars that floated out when she shifted.

The woman had a flowered wreath on her head, and long curling hair that fell down around her pointed ears and rounded shoulders. She stretched her hand out to Morgan and said, "Come."

Morgan blinked, then found herself at the elf woman's side.

"My name is Rebekah. Come with me."

"To where?" Morgan questioned.

"On an adventure, if you wish to find your heart again, we must recover what you've hidden underneath years of hurt, hate and scarring."

Morgan watched Rebekah turn away.

Her hair was long and golden, flowing almost to her knees. Her skin was smooth and fair and her eyes were sea foam green.

Morgan took a step delicately and watched the spot below her foot infect the area with lush green grass. It spread as far as she could see. A blue sky was unrolled far and flowers bloomed high above the tall reeds starting to blow. A butterfly floated by and

Morgan heard a little girl laughing beyond her reach. Morgan looked around, but didn't see the elf, Rebekah. Morgan pushed her way through the overgrowth until she discovered a little girl sprawled out in a flattened area. She wore a pretty dress with an apron.

Morgan recognized her as herself.

She got up and danced around, laughing.

She turned around and saw Morgan watching, picked a flower, and offered it to her.

"Come on, come play with me!"

"Ok..."

Morgan put the daisy behind her ear and chased after the child.

Really, she was chasing after herself.

Morgan leapt like a cricket through the grass, laughing as she tried to catch the fleeing figure in front of her.

The two stopped, linked hands, and spun around and around until the scenery blurred together like a runny rainbow.

Morgan noticed she was spinning by herself now. She turned around and saw a dark green, unicorn-like horse, and Rebekah holding the reins.

"Come take a ride with me, I have something to show you."

Morgan stepped forward and took the worn rope from the woman's hand.

She alighted and positioned herself to ride. The horse galloped at full speed through the field and into the woods.

Morgan laughed heartily as she felt the wind tickle her face.

She held tight to the mare's mane and looked around the enchanted forest.

The trees were tall and their roots grew down into a blue swamp. The waters were clean and beautiful. The trees branches leaned over and dripped into the puddles gracefully. The roots were heaved up and twisted, making high spots on the ground. Soon the forest thinned and they traveled onto a beach.

The horse slowed to a trot as Morgan listened to the rhythm of the waves crash back and forth on the rocks.

Morgan noticed a boy, about her age, standing on the rocks. He threw stones into the breaking waves.

Morgan halted the horse and ran down the beach after him. She got to the shoreline and lost sight of him.

"Hello?" she called out.

"Rebekah?"

"Anyone, anyone out here?"

Then she felt a strong hand gently slip into hers. She looked down at it as it pulled her along the beach.

Morgan ran hard, not letting go.

She felt the salty water splash her face and refresh her spirit.

She spread her arms out wide and screamed at the top of her

lungs.

She looked over and noticed her mysterious companion was gone. He had vanished.

Morgan slowly walked to a river that emptied out into the ocean. It was flowing fast and smoothly.

"Upon the river the rocks fall…"

Morgan turned and saw Rebekah standing in the waters. The current pulled the train of her long flowing gown.

"The large jagged ones are rough and hollow, until they are stabbed into the sand."

Morgan looked down into the water.

"The raging waters flow through, causing you. The deepest part of you becomes smooth. Those deep jagged parts, the sharpest sides are smoothed away by the river. Now they are smoother, they've been made better by I Am."

Morgan lifted a small, smooth stone out of the passing waters. She felt her fingers travel over its entire surface.

"Only by the river, God, can your stone be made smooth."

Morgan placed her hand into the river, palm up, so the stone turned over and was carried away.

She gazed at her reflection thoughtfully. Then she saw a long white stairway down through the clouds. Morgan found herself wearing a long white dress with flowing sleeves and a ruffled edge. She lifted the bottom of the silken gown, letting the back trail behind.

A light breeze blew into her face from below, letting her hair rise up and whip around in tiny strands.

As the fog cleared, she found a bedroom below. She floated through the air and walked over to a bed.

In the bed was the boy she was on the beach with.

"I'm here," she said to the sleeper.

She bent over his face and stroked his hair.

He had dark, thick hair and pale skin. His hands were worn and tired looking.

Morgan felt she knew him, and to leave him would only vex her more. She didn't want to leave.

A tear dropped from her face as the edges faded away. Things became darker as she called "I know you…"

Then things grew darker. Then all was black as night.

"I've dreamt in my life dreams, dreams that have stayed with me ever after, and changed my ideas ; They've gone through and through me like wine through water, and altered the colour of my mind.

- Emily Bronte

~ Chapter Thirty–Five ~

~ Chapter Thirty-Five ~

Morgan turned around and found sand all around her. Sand pummeled her face and penetrated every fiber of her clothing.

"Rebekah! Help!" she screamed.

Morgan looked up at the hot sun, blocked by the fierce sand storm.

Morgan realized she was in a layered outfit. She wore a shirt with lace, a peasant skirt, and a lightweight overskirt wrapped around that. She had a patterned shawl and scarf over her hair and face.

Morgan covered her nose and walked against the wind.

She fell onto her face and tried to keep her balance. Scratching at the hot sand, Morgan cried out in pain and frustration, knowing she wasn't going anywhere.

Then she looked up through the curtain of sand and dust and a figure stood before her in the distance.

Strong arms came forward and scooped her up onto a white Arabian horse.

Through the raging storm, the rider carried Morgan for what seemed like miles.

Then Morgan looked out upon the horizon and saw a village.

She turned around to see his face, but in shock, she saw the man had a black turban and mask. Morgan tried to pull back, but he had a strong grip.

The man pulled her into a tent with several women in burkahs and some Arabian swordsmen. An older man with a white beard sat on a pile of silk pillows with oriental rugs all around.

Some urns and flasks of oil were on intricately carved wooden tables.

Morgan's heart thumped wildly as she saw the fighters walk towards her.

"On your feet, woman," one commanded.

She stood up, and was shackled to a support beam.

The five men went into the corner to the important man to talk.

The women stared at her in shame.

She became worried; she did not want to be here.

The men then turned and spoke to her.

"Who is your father?"

"My father?" she questioned.

One of the men stepped forward threateningly.

"He asked you a question, answer it!"

"Is he Ali Kurktan?"

"No."

"Benezar?"

"Nooo…"

"What about Sayed Selim?"

"No, I don't know any of these names!" Morgan screamed in a panic.

The men turned away and grunted.

Suddenly a bright light appeared in the tent; it grew and grew, until it took the form of a girl about the age of fourteen. She had bright blue eyes that could pierce your soul.

She had delicate wings on her back and a short tunic.

"My name is Keturah, my duty is to show you many adventures."

"Adventure? This is not adventure!"

Morgan gestured to the chain around her wrist.

"Just trust me… believe in destiny…"

The girl faded back into a dim light, then vanished.

"So this is all an illusion of my imagination?" Morgan asked herself.

"If I'm going to make this an 'adventure', I should try to play a part, or make a story through my actions.

Morgan jumped up and pulled at her shackles.

"Release me! I'm the daughter of a wealthy king!"

The men turned in disbelief.

"Then what is his name?"

"Uh…"

The men laughed and shoved Morgan back down onto the soft carpeting.

"Leave my presence," the old man ordered.

So the men left.

"I am the sultan, and you are not my daughter, nor the daughter of Arabia. Tell me your name, young maiden."

"Morgan."

"You must be sent away from here, this is not your place."

"Why do you say that?"

"Do not question me!" the man demanded, turning in disgust.

"You are not dark, you are not of this realm."

Morgan nodded in confirmation.

Morgan heard a horse ride up and swords clash outside.

The women rose and ran in fear.

Morgan listened is disbelief as dozens of men fell and died at the hand of one rider. His shadow showed him to be young as well.

The sultan got up, grabbed a blade, and ran forward.

The mysterious swordsman sliced a hole down the side of the tent and charged in.

He wore a veil over his face and a vest and sash. His pants ballooned out like the rest of the men, but they were dirty and ripped. The two fighters clashed their blades and danced around the tent, ducking and jumping over pillows.

The young man leaped and spun around with extreme talent.

He displayed such grace, as if he were dancing in a ballet. The two continued fiercely fighting until the sultan missed his timing and got sliced across the abdomen. He stared at the masked man, then fell on his back in silence.

The man put his sword back in his sheath, then slowly walked over to Morgan.

Her heart beat like a tribal drum.

He bent down and examined her chains.

She stared at him and blinked slowly.

Things seemed to be in slow motion as he gazed into her eyes.

He pulled his sword out and lifted it over his head, ready to strike.

Morgan pulled back and screamed in fear as he let his blade fall onto a chain link, breaking Morgan's shackles.

He knelt back down and stared at her again. She looked deeply into his dark brown eyes and smiles. He was here to rescue her.

They tore out of the tent and jumped onto his stallion.

He let his sword out and whipped past insurgents all around.

Morgan could almost hear the rhythmic drums and Arabic chants over the horizon of the setting sun.

The horse clomped long and hard into the sunset as the two leaned steady over the racing beast.

The rescuer whipped the reins hard and yelled "yah, yah!" as he turned and looked behind him to see a cloud of dust from a group of pursuers on horses.

Morgan was the source of the adventure, and the heart of his bravery. They turned onto a camel path and up a rocky ravine. He stopped the horse and took Morgan by the waist and pulled her close. With his other hand, he gripped the back of her neck.

Morgan felt a flood of mysterious dessert romance sweep over her as she closed her eyes.

When she opened them, her rider was gone.

Morgan let a sad tear fall from her face.

"I didn't even know his name."

"Who, my lady?"

Morgan turned to find a maidservant behind her.

She looked around and found herself standing in a gray stone tower.

She observed a tiara was on her head and her hair was in one long braid.

She wore a long, red velvet dress with a belt that fell down around her hips. Her sleeves were wide and flowing, covering her hands completely. The top was a low swoop neck collar with a gold pattern down the front.

"The man who rescued me," Morgan answered.

"We all dream to be rescued by a wealthy Lord, my mistress."

Morgan nodded in agreement and turned away, fleeing down a winding staircase to a bedroom. This room was also gray stone, but a large wooden carved canopy bed with furs on it laid in the center. A vanity table and fire pit were to the side.

More animal furs were placed randomly around the room.

Morgan threw herself on the bed and cried. She finally got up and went over to a small window; it was a long and narrow cut out in the organized block pattern.

Out over the large full moon, a rider could be seen.

"Crusader!" Morgan heard a guard call out.

Morgan whipped up the stairs to her high tower. The wind blew her dress fiercely, but she stood tall to the approaching Noble.

His horse galloped through the gate and out of Morgan's sight.

She flew back down the stairs and into her room. A long jeweled saber sword laid on a mantle on the wall.

Morgan gripped it in her hands, getting a feel for her strength. She maneuvered a little, then raced down the stone stairway, leading to the first floor, with her chosen weapon.

A man in full armor turned and blocked her exit, so she raised her sword and hit him on the head. A large dent was in his helmet as he fell unconscious.

Morgan ran down the hall as dogs followed after her. She laughed in pure excitement as the sound of steel clashing together could be heard.

More soldiers appeared in the large hall she entered.

They drew their swords and challenged Morgan.

"Princess!" someone screamed.

Morgan turned to see, but a sword came down near her shoulder.

She side stepped the blade and glided past. Glorious music could be heard in her head as enemies fell all around, some at her own hand.

Soon she could see the man who came through the gate.

He wore tight tan leggings and brown buckled boots. A long-sleeved robe was under a bright colored sash wound around his shoulder and waist. The robe and sash fell to about his knees. A jewel at his collar held the sash in place, and a belt-like buckle was fastened across his chest. He had a cloth sheath and belt over all of that.

His long hair flowed as he moved.

He turned and met Morgan's gaze. She then realized it was her rescuer. She called out to him as resistors fell all around him.

"You have been following me?"

"Yes, I will go through hell and fire to find you!" he called back.

His voice was low and smooth as velvet.

He reached over and grabbed Morgan's hand.

"My love." He finished.

Morgan gripped his arm as he moved in an agile way out the door.

They ran from the open gate and down the dirt path.

Morgan felt the heavy cloth fly behind her as they fled the castle.

He veered off into the woods and slowly crept under vines.

Morgan looked around the eerie woodlands and swamp.

"Where is your horse?" she asked in fear.

"Say nothing!" he commanded.

Immediately Morgan heard the growl of a sinister beast. The noise grew louder as she heard swamp puddles slosh and a creature scream at the smell of live flesh.

Morgan screeched and the man drew his sword, grabbed Morgan's sleeve, and ran.

"My horse is up here- Zenith! Come!"

To Morgan's amazement, a horse came around the corner.

It had no saddle or blanket; it was pure shining white, bigger than she had ever seen.

It whinnied and rose up on its hind feet as light poured into the dark swamp. Morgan was thrown up onto the horse and led away.

"Wait, no!" she screamed.

"I will come back for you!" he promised, as dark eyes slunk through the swamp.

"I don't even know you, what is your name?" she screamed, trying to turn back around.

"Jack."

"Have you ever dreamt it would be this way?"

- Ashley Lauren Boettcher

~ Chapter Thirty-Six ~

~ Chapter Thirty-Six ~

"Jack," Morgan repeated to herself.

Then Morgan looked around to find new surroundings. She knew she was in Victorian London.

There were carriages all around, and policemen guided the congested cobblestone streets.

Women with bonnets and baskets rushed around feeling fruits at grocery stands and boys in cabby hats ran around laughing.

Morgan closed her eyes and created a similar outfit as the women she saw, in her mind. She looked down and opened her eyes.

It worked.

She now wore a long dress buttoned down the front, with three-quarter sleeves ruffled at the end and around the neckline. A large red tie was clipped on the front and the back of her dress was pulled up and puckered. The waist was tight and had seams that followed down to the hips, making a corset-like top.

She had a bustle above the gathered cloth and her hair was in a loose bun.

Morgan tarried along the road and hopped up onto the sidewalk.

"I know I'll see Jack, I just have to find him."

Morgan passed a newspaper stand.

The date on top said:

August 16th, 1892

Morgan smiled and picked it up, some critics made her laugh, how unknowledgeable people were in this time.

Morgan walked down the busy street and found a doll store.

She walked in and saw many mechanical dolls, puppets, train sets, and sailboats.

There were beautiful porcelain dolls dressed as brides, schoolgirls or just plain dolls in popular fashion. Morgan walked over to a small shelf with music boxes on it.

One song was playing- the lullaby!

Morgan picked up the wooden instrument and found it to be the same one she owned. Morgan turned it over and realized it was the same one.

An identical scratch on the bottom of the box she owned was on the one she held.

Morgan put the box down and stepped back.

Morgan turned away and walked out the door.

The busy streets were gone, now it was dark as night.

Keturah stood in front of her, smiling, and Morgan had returned to her normal clothes.

"You see, dreams hold many adventures, if you let them."

"But I don't see what it has to do with anything here, I mean, who is Jack, and why Arabia?"

The fairy girl smiled wider.

"You explain it, this is your dream."

Morgan had completely forgotten, she held the remote to this film playing in her head.

"Perhaps you don't fully understand."

She turned away and faded into the blackness.

"Wait! Keturah!"

Morgan tried to follow her, but she had turned into dust and floated up into the starlit sky.

Morgan noticed a small glowing frame appearing. It formed into a window-like structure, with objects and people inside.

Actually, a person, just one.

Morgan cautiously walked over to the window and looked inside.

An old woman was sitting in a rocking chair, sewing. She had a fire burning and some dinner left over on the plate. The left over plate setting was for just one. One chair sat at the table, and the woman looked as if she were lonely. She frowned at the cloth she was pulling the needle in and out of. Obviously, she had a hard life, alone and unwanted.

Then the window faded away.

A person in white walked gracefully toward her.

Morgan couldn't tell if it was a man or a woman; its facial features consisted of both, and it had hair that flowed down to about shoulder length. Large feathered wings rose up from behind its back. A sword was stuck in the robes' belt he or she wore.

It took her arm gently and guided her through the darkness and into the room Morgan was looking into.

"This is you," it said.

Morgan was shocked. This woman lived alone, unmarried.

"I wept because I had no shoes, until I saw a man who had no feet."

- Persian Proverb

~ Chapter Thirty-Seven ~

"Count your Blessings" Wise Words Woman's Day Magazine November 18th 2003 67th year issue #1 page 160

~ Chapter Thirty-Seven ~

The Angel guided Morgan to the doorway and let her inside. The old woman apparently could not see them because she didn't look up at the sight of the two.

"If you do not change, this will be your fate."

"An old maid?!" Morgan asked doubtfully.

"God has a design for your life, and you have strayed from that path, against the tide. Now your future holds no miracles."

"Miracles?"

"Yes, your life is a miracle, and you have denied that truth, you question God's plan and try to rip the plans from His hand."

"But I prayed. I gave my life over!" Morgan protested.

"In words… yes. In will, no."

"What is that supposed to mean?"

"You may speak good intent, but obviously you don't plan on living it."

The Angel gestured toward the crippled old woman.

"This is a definite future?"

"No, you must change your ways."

"How do I do that?" Morgan asked.

"Depend on God. Offer every fiber of yourself to Him, and your life will be whole."

Whole… Morgan had never thought she would ever become whole, maybe left with a hole…

"How will I grow up if I can change?" Morgan asked desperately.

"Let me show you," the Angel answered.

The room faded and another scene appeared before her.

Morgan looked around and saw a church with many people; at the front were bridesmaids and groomsmen, a minister and a groom himself, though Morgan couldn't make out his face.

The bridesmaids wore dark burgundy and wine colored gowns and held pink and yellow lilies.

Morgan started walking up the aisle. The audience rose and stared at her.

She continued to walk gracefully towards her groom. Excitement grew inside her as he took her delicate hand into his.

It was worn and strong.

Morgan looked up and gazed into his dark brown eyes. He smiled, letting a tear fall down his cheek.

Morgan knew him; it was her rescuer, Jack.

This was her future, this was her love.

Morgan was determined to have this; she wanted happiness and love, not just for herself.

She wanted other girls like her to feel the happiness redemption a future brought. She wanted a ministry.

Morgan turned away from Jack and faced the Angel.

"I see now."

"See what?" it asked.

"That happiness isn't about what I can get to satisfy me."

"Indeed."

"Only God can supply happiness, so I need to look to Him, and fulfill myself in Him and in return, I'll have a secure future."

"Yes."

Morgan looked around and saw she was back in a dark nothing.

Stars were above and below her, and all around her.

Rebekah and Keturah now stood next to the Angel.

"Your journey is over," Rebekah commented.

"You mean the Book of Dreams?"

"Yes, you have fulfilled your dream, you have it, and it's yours."

"Now go," Keturah commanded.

Morgan stepped backwards and turned away.

She laid comfortably in her bed. A light breeze filled the air, spreading a pleasant scent. Morgan ran her hands along the soft white fabric on the place she lay. Morgan turned her head and listened with her eyes closed, to someone walking in. Morgan felt the presence of someone standing over her.

She opened her eyes and saw Jack.

He sat down at her side and stroked her face lightly.

Morgan closed her eyes and smiled.

"I love you more than fish love the sea, Morgan," he said.

Morgan opened her eyes and gazed at him in wonder.

"That's beautiful."

"No, you are."

Jack leaned to kiss Morgan. She closed her eyes and touched his face.

Morgan felt content with this passionate embrace. It was like eternity to her, she forgot about her mistakes, how she gave a kiss away at the drop of a hat, how she let her body be used as a mere toy, this was how it was supposed to be; this was love; this was forever.

Morgan opened her eyes and looked into his. They were so bright, so clear, so lovely. Morgan heard thunder roll in the distance and a raindrop hit her face.

Rain fell down onto the couch. Morgan looked around to find she was in a garden.

"I didn't see that before," she thought.

Jack laid down beside her and embraced her. Morgan closed her eyes and slept comfortably. She dreamt pleasant dreams, dreams of adventure and love.

"I know that time brings change
and change takes time."

- Nichole Nordemen

~ Chapter Thirty-Eight ~

~ Chapter Thirty-Eight ~

Morgan opened her eyes and heard birds singing and street noise.

Morgan immediately sat up.

Three burnt out candles were on the floor next to an old book.

It was on its last page.

The words were faded and curvy.

Morgan leaned in and read:

"You are only what you dream to be."

Morgan smiled widely. She knew what her dream was, and she would get it.

Morgan's junior year in high school rushed by fast, where she worked hard and managed to get a couple of A's.

Now summer had rolled around again, and she had her whole summer, and her whole life ahead of her.

"So, what do you think it will be like?" Morgan asked Mia, as they walked down the street.

"I think it should be very hot this time of year."

"It's probably hot all year long," Morgan contradicted.

"What is the main goal for the missions team?"

"Well, we are building a church, and just visiting some of the villages, getting a feel for the people, what it's like to live in India."

"I'm so exited for you!" Mia squealed, squeezing Morgan's hand.

"Well, I have to get back home, mom and Jay have a dinner reservation tonight."

"Speaking of…" Mia hinted.

"Huh?" Morgan asked.

"Well, Ryan and I…"

"No way!"

"Yes way!"

"You and Ryan are going out?"

"Really, we have been for a while, but we never regarded each other as boyfriend and girlfriend. Everyone else thought we were, and you know, we are such good friends…"

"Wow, I'm stunned."

"Why?" Mia asked.

"Because I knew it last August."

"How?!"

"I saw Ryan looking at you during my birthday party, and it was a look," Morgan recalled.

"Hmm…"

"Ok, well, um, talk to me later, call or something!" Morgan called, walking the other way."

"Ok! Have fun with Adam!" Mia yelled back.

Morgan rolled her eyes and laughed as she ran back down the street.

Morgan climbed up the apartment steps and into the kitchen.

"Hey mom, hey Jay."

"Hi hon," her mom answered.

"We're going to head out now, you guys be good," Jay said laughing.

"Sure," Morgan stated flatly, chomping a bite out of her apple.

Adam came in and poured some juice.

"When are you coming home?"

"About…" Jay began, then interrupted himself.

"After you go to sleep."

"No fair!" he stamped his foot and pretended to pout.

All three laughed and Mrs. Parker and James left.

Morgan left for her mission trip to India in one week. This was an adventure Morgan had anticipated for a long time.

It made her think of the book, and of grandma. She thanked grandma for this book, this life changing experience, which she couldn't quite understand.

Morgan didn't know if she fell asleep while reading, started day dreaming while reading these stories, or the adventures were real and truly supernatural. Completely unexplainable, but what she did know was grandma had had the same experience and blessed Morgan with the opportunity to change her life, even after she left her own.

Morgan saw love all around: Mia and Ryan, mom and Jay, grandpa and Liana, a very nice woman he met, Morgan figured it was at Bingo.

Regardless, she expected it soon; she yearned for the chance to meet Jack.

"Will I see him in a crowd and know it's him?"

"Will he see me and know who I am?" Morgan thought.

"Did he share my dream? Will he remember those?"

Morgan didn't know the answers, but God did.

"I lie awake, and I am like a
sparrow alone on the housetop."
- Psalm 102:7

~ Chapter Thirty-Nine ~

~ Chapter Thirty-Nine ~

Morgan heard her mom come back home at 11:15 pm. Morgan got up and went into the dark kitchen to greet her mom.

She was crying.

"Mom! What's the matter?" Morgan asked, rushing over.

"Turn on the light," she ordered.

Morgan flicked on the light and sat down at the table with her mother.

"Jay told me his amazing life story and transformation."

Morgan knew he had tried to witness to her, but she was probably crying because she refused to listen and so they broke up. Morgan clenched her teeth at the thought.

"Hon, it was amazing, that's the only word I can use to describe it, because now I understand you."

Morgan looked at her, perplexed.

"Huh?"

"I understand you, I feel the same way you do."

"Explain this to me," Morgan answered.

"All my life, mom was always, in my eyes, the 'Holier-than-thou' type, and then you, and when I found out James was a Christian too, I began to question my faith." She smiled excitedly.

"He talked to me and explained some things and we just sat for hours after dinner, just talking. Then he popped the question."

Morgan sat up straight in her seat.

"What was that last part?" she asked nervously.

"He asked me to marry him."

Tears ran down her cheek as an angelic smile flooded her face.

"I know he's 'the one'."

"He is," Morgan agreed.

"So you approve?" her mom asked excitedly.

"Yes, I may have felt this way all along, I don't know why, I just do."

"Oh hon, you make me so happy!" she complimented, hugging Morgan tightly.

She showed Morgan her diamond ring in the dim light. The moon shining in made it glisten and shine brilliantly.

"Congratulations, mom."

"Thank you honey."

The two went into their rooms, happy. Morgan was glad for her mom, and for herself, life was finally straightening out. Sarah was glad that she would have a husband and father her children loved just as much as she did, one who would support her financially and spiritually; she never had that before.

Morgan stared at the ceiling reflectively.

"I give my life wholly to you," Morgan chanted quietly.

"Everything I have is yours, bless this marriage too, and please make it yours."

Then Morgan fell asleep.

Morgan got up early the next morning. She dressed in a pair of worn jeans and a tank.

She climbed up onto the roof and looked out over the horizon.

"This must have been like what Moses felt when he saw the Promised Land," she said.

"My life is speeding along so quickly God, please, give me a purpose."

Morgan leaned on the stone wall and stared down at the street.

She was alone, solitary, and happy in this complete silence. She wouldn't have it any other way.

Morgan turned around and went back down into her apartment.

Jay was there.

"Hey Morgan!"

He called her over.

"I heard about your engagement."

The youth pastor looked at her expectantly.

"And I'm happy!"

Her mother smiled widely and continued sifting through the mail.

"Well I'm glad," Jay added.

"When will plans start?" Morgan asked.

"Probably this fall, for an early spring wedding."

"I like April," Morgan's mom commented.

"Right."

Jay gestured to Sarah like "she's the boss."

Morgan laughed and left the room.

They celebrated that night with a big dinner and cake. Then Morgan went to a movie with Ryan, Angela, and Mia.

She got home at midnight, right at her curfew.

Morgan popped her head into Adam's room and found he was sleeping soundly.

She rounded to corner and shut her door quietly.

In the quiet of her room, Morgan found comfort in a votive candle flickering in the dimness, and a small music box to remind her that she wasn't alone.

"In the spring a young mans fancy
lightly turns to thoughts of love."
- Alfred, Lord Tennyson

~ Chapter Forty ~

*Wise Words "Welcome Spring" Woman's Day Magazine
March 4th 2003 66th year 6th issue page 248*

~ Chapter Forty ~

Light poured into Morgan's room. Saturday morning traffic noise plowed through the bedroom windows.

Morgan yawned and stretched her arms like a bungee cord, letting them snap back.

Adam and her mom were up in the kitchen cleaning up the dishes when the phone rang.

"Hello?" Morgan asked.

"Morgan, can you come over?" Mia asked.

"Sure, why?"

"Ryan is bringing his friend from South Africa over, we are all planning to go out to lunch and show him New York City, if you can come."

"Let me ask…"

Morgan covered the phone with her hand and explained the situation to her mom.

"I don't see why not, just bring the cell phone to be safe."

"It's cool," Morgan told Mia.

"Great, be at my house in, hmm… about an hour and a half."

"Ok, bye!"

"Bye!" Mia called excitedly as Morgan hung up.

Morgan poured herself some juice and hurried over to her room and opened the closet door.

She pulled out a pair of shorts and a loose tee shirt.

She slipped on her sneakers and ran out the door.

"Morgan!" her mom called.

Morgan looked up the steps to the kitchen door.

"Forget something?" she asked, tossing the cell phone.

"Thanks!" Morgan said, racing back down the stairs.

She jogged to Mia's house and arrived ten minutes early.

Morgan slowed her pace and stepped up to the door.

Mia answered immediately.

"They here yet?"

"No. They should, soon, or we'll miss the next ferry to Ellis Island!" Mia commented agitated.

Angela walked in an offered a snack to Morgan so they could eat while they waited.

Then the girls heard the doorbell.

Ryan and his friend walked in happily.

"Everyone," Ryan started.

"This is Jack Warner; he's going to be a senior here this year."

"Oh my Lord." Morgan breathed out.

Jack Warner was tall and muscular; he had brown hair and piercing hazel eyes. He had rough, hardworking hands and wore a pair of worn jeans and a jacket.

"He turned seventeen just last month." Ryan commented.

Jack's gaze met Morgan's.

Their eyes stayed locked as the others conversation continued.

Morgan's heart soared as he slowly walked towards her.

"I'm Jack," he introduced himself.

"Morgan, but… I think you know that," Morgan whispered.

Jack tilted his head and beamed.

"I think this could be the start of something special."

"I think it already is," Morgan spat out.

"Ya ready?" Angela asked the two.

"Where are we going to?" Jack asked.

"The Statue of Liberty; we have to hurry, or we'll miss the ferry!" Mia said, grabbing her jacket.

The five walked out onto the sidewalk. As Ryan and Mia took each other's hands, Jack slowed his pace to walk by Morgan's side, in the back.

"So you are seventeen as well?"

"I will be in August."

"Ahh…"

"Have you ever been to South Africa?"

"I'm going on a trip to India this month, but I haven't been to Africa at all."

"It's beautiful there," Jack commented.

"You should have a trip there someday."

Morgan smiled and thought to herself, "I just may."

Morgan's mind wandered to thoughts of India as she handed her ticket to the woman at the boarding ramp.

Jack would be waiting for her when she got back.

"Seat 16, row 35, hon."

Morgan wheeled her bag over the crack between the floor and the plane. She found her seat, a window seat, and thrust her bag under the chair. She sat down and took a deep breath; this would change her life. Not only was this her first plane flight, this was her first time overseas, and on a mission's trip. This was what would get the wheel turning, the arrows to point the way, to show her true destiny.

Eight hours later, Morgan's legs ached and the food clashed on the tray.

"Please clear your folding trays and put your seats in their upright position," the attendant declared over the intercom.

Morgan passed her plate to the smiling woman collecting soda and meals. Morgan then put her seatbelt on.

The attendant checked their seats and the plane landed.

Morgan looked out at the dusty runway as the plane docked.

This was like nothing she had ever seen; it was like being in a different world.

Morgan collected her stuff and grabbed her carry-on and walked down a flight of stairs that led out onto the runway itself.

There to meet her was a little girl with snarled hair and dark skin. She had hoop earrings and a skirt on. She had no shoes or shirt though. Her arms and legs were like pencils and her stomach stuck out like a balloon was implanted under her skin.

Morgan felt tears in her eyes, she loved this little girl, because in some ways, she reminded her of herself, and Morgan was overjoyed to know she could change this little girl's life forever.

She knew she had found her dream.

"All, everything that I understand,
I understand because I love."

- Leo Tolstoy

~ Chapter Forty-One ~

~ Chapter Forty-One ~

"And do you, Pastor James Cole, take Sarah May Parker to be your wife?"

"I do."

Morgan leaned forward as she watched Jay and Sarah kiss.

She was the maid-of-honor for her mother's April wedding, which she was happy to be.

Her two-week mission trip was amazing and she got to know a lot about this different culture and how to be a hard worker.

110 degrees in the sun, building a church was work, but wearing traditional woman's apparel during the rest of the day was hard.

She couldn't stop talking about it, even after eight months.

At the reception, Morgan sat with Jack and Angela.

"That was a great ceremony," Angela commented.

"It was awesome," Morgan returned.

Jack took her hand and kissed it.

"Would you like to dance to this song?"

Morgan listened and heard an oldies tune playing.

She couldn't say no.

Morgan and Jack got onto the dance floor and swayed to the music gracefully.

"What will you do when you graduate?" Jack asked.

"I'm definitely going to go to a Bible college. I want to start an inner city ministry for teen girls."

"That is great!"

"I feel it's my calling."

Morgan looked down at her feet sadly.

"When are you going back home?"

"In July," he answered.

"Are you ever coming back?"

Jack lifted Morgan's chin and met her eyes.

"I have two more years of school there, and I could visit in the summer, but you know what, I love it here, I'm going back to get approval to move to the United States."

Morgan's chin dropped.

"Permission from your parents?"

He nodded.

"Wow, uh, why?"

Jack smiled and stroked the top of Morgan's head.

"I wouldn't leave you, I've dreamt about you."

Morgan's heart jumped.

"You have?"

"Yes, many times."

"I never wanted to tell anyone this, but I have too…"

Morgan hesitated.

"Dreamt about you."

Jack stopped dancing and stared at her.

"I knew you before we met, I was in love with you before we met."

Jack smiled, went back to dancing slowly, and said, "I've loved you my whole life, and I will for the rest that will come."

Morgan let a tear fall onto the dance floor.

"I don't know what to say, Jack, I love you."

"And I love you, Morgan Parker."

Everything in Morgan wished to hear more words on the end.

Just four more precious words, but they didn't come.

A week later, in Mia's room, Morgan retold her story.

"It will happen Morgan, it has to!"

Morgan sighed and threw herself onto the bed.

"No man moves across the world to another continent for a girl he doesn't plan on marrying," she added.

Morgan considered this.

"I just wish I were out of school and farther along in life so we could get married."

"God set this up, He's got His reasons, so concentrate on school right now, Jack isn't going anywhere."

"I'm afraid it won't work."

"Morgan, you need to stop doubting, you didn't dream about him because he would be your friend for a year and then disappear. God chose him as your husband, he's 'the one.'"

Morgan smiled and sprawled out on the bed.

"I know he is."

Mia shifted in her seat and leaned toward Morgan.

"Ryan is too… we're getting married."

Morgan screamed and flew over to Mia.

"When? Oh my God, when?" she shrieked.

"After we graduate, obviously, and sometime after he's found a university."

"Wow, it's amazing, we grew up so fast."

"I never wanted to."

"Wanted what?" Morgan asked.

"To grow up so fast. I wanted to stay young, like you, to be able to stay with my childhood forever."

"I didn't have the best childhood, Mia, you know that."

"But you found something good about it, and you held on to it, you fought for its life and that's what makes you!"

Morgan stared out the window in a daze.

"No, God fought for my life, that's what made me who I am now."

Mia turned around and smiled.

"Amen."

"What you are is Gods gift to you; what you do with yourself is your gift to God."

- *Danish Proverb*

~ Chapter Forty-Two ~

~ Chapter Forty-Two ~

Morgan walked over to her terminal reluctantly.

"Well, I'm off to Moody Bible College," Morgan sighed.

Angela stepped forward and hugged her, while Mia and Ryan stood behind Morgan's parents.

"Call us when you get there!" Morgan's mom called out.

"I will."

Morgan turned to Jack and gave him a big hug.

"I'll miss you so much..." she sobbed.

"Morgan, this is the next step up the stairway, remember?" Jack asked.

"She would have loved to see this!"

"I'm sure she does," Jack commented.

"Only 112 days until you come home again!" he encouraged.

Morgan sniffled out a laugh and turned to board.

"I love you all, guys!"

Then she left, for the most incredible journey of her life.

Though it wasn't as many thousands of miles as India, it was still Chicago, away from home and away from Jack.

When Morgan got into the airport, she felt right at home, outside was like she was in New York City again.

"Thank you, God, I wouldn't be able to do this if I weren't in a city again."

Morgan's SAT score was relatively high and she made good grades in high school.

She no longer had the menacing voice telling her that she never could. Morgan had confidence in herself, without confidence in God, she would be right back where she was.

In reality, she was nothing, worthless, and unwanted, but God made her into something, worthwhile, He wanted her, and that was like a dream come true.

"...Unless a grain of wheat falls into the ground and dies, it remains alone; but if it dies, it produces much grain. He who loves his life will lose it, and he who hates his life in this world, will keep it for eternal life. If anyone serves Me, let him follow Me; and where I am, there my servant will be also. If anyone serves Me, him My Father will honor."

(John 12:24-26)

So Morgan's journey began; really, it didn't begin when she was born, it didn't begin when she got on that plane, it didn't start when she got to school, or when she met Jack. It started on that warm June evening, in the pouring rain, in the thundering voice of God.

Morgan found her purpose when she stood on the bridge and let go of everything she had, everything she was or ever could be.

It began when she discovered that dreams really do come true, that there is a happy ending, after all.

"You told me who I am, I am Yours."

- "Casting Crowns"

~ Epilogue ~

~ Epilogue ~

When Morgan returned home after school she had a missions degree and started a teen girls program called "TIC" (Teens inner city program) established after only two years.

Mom and Jay had a baby boy, Nathaniel. Mia and Ryan got married the year of Morgan's 21st birthday. Adam was class president in his first year of Jr. High, and was an honor roll student for three more years. Angela moved to China as a full time missionary leader, she never married.

Now, as for Jack and Morgan, they got married. Morgan Parker-Warner married when she was twenty three and had two girls, Anna and Christina, and a baby boy named Daniel.

Morgan secretly loved the name "Daniel" because Daniel was a dreamer, he was a hero in the end, and he became a great man.

Morgan touched the stars that seemed so distant. She was a dreamer too, and she hoped with her life's story, she helped others dare to dream too.

If you have never...

Given your life over to Christ, or you feel like you have wandered away in your relationship with Him, don't feel rejected and forgotten. Like Morgan, God is just waiting for you to realize He has been there all along.

If you are willing to take a step towards forgiveness and a life grounded in truth, pray.......

"Dear Father, thank you for showing me I am not as worthless as I think, that You thought I was valuable enough to suffer and die, taking my place on the cross, and taking my sins.

I accept the forgiveness You have offered me, and I reject my old ways. Help me to get back to a place where I can recognize Your face, and be able to call You my Dad!

I believe that You did die, thinking only of me, and I believe that You rose victorious, after death.

I know that someday I will join You in heaven, and enjoy being in Your company forever.

Purify me, refine me, and help me to follow You, and do everything to reflect You. Fill me with the love You have shown me, and help me to lead others to Your perfect truth.

I love You- In Jesus' name, Amen."

If you prayed that prayer, find a church or friend who can help you grow.

I dream that someday, we will meet, and praise Jesus for the dreams He gives to us....

Jeremiah 29:11-13
"...Call Upon Me..."